Campus

Campus Menace

Preston Shires

Campus Menace
Preston Shires

Copyright © 2020 Preston Shires

All rights reserved.

ISBN: 9798687014137
Independently published

DEDICATION

To the Memory of Anthony (Toney) McCrann
1940-2006
Professor of English, Peru State College

I admired Toney's breadth of knowledge and his
insightful wit, but more importantly,
I experienced his spiritual honesty and the
generosity of his heart.

This book is a work of fiction.

Names, characters, and events are the product of the author's imagination or are used fictitiously. Any resemblance to situations, locales, or persons, living or dead, is coincidental.

CHARACTERS

STUDENTS
- Angela likes books, studies, and scholarships.
- Barton likes parties and just having a good time everywhere.
- Cambria likes Jesus and lets everyone know about it.
- Franky is something of a nerd, certainly socially awkward.
- Quinton is a religious skeptic and lets everyone know about it.
- Stanley is very particular about housekeeping, but strong as an ox.
- Tasia is very proud of having won a beauty pageant.

FACULTY
- Alfred 'Al' Tate: Professor of Drama
- Henry Langstrom: Professor of History
- Sonia Abbot: Professor of Sociology
- Simeon 'Sim' Garfield: Professor of Political Science
- Tristan Telsmith: Adjunct Professor of History

PRESIDENT OF ASPINWALL COLLEGE
- Dr. Larimer

1

Saturday, October 10

Normally, Saturday mornings rank just as high as a Sunday morning, even higher, when considering they're not followed by a Monday. But this Saturday morning lost all its promise at nine a.m., when Cambria Davenport came rapping at my chamber door, or rather at my chamber window.

It's not that I totally despise Cambria, she exhibits certain physical attributes that a young bachelor must not disregard. She's blond, but not in a fake way, has bright blue eyes, usually set behind the lenses of some thickish reading glasses, and possesses a prominent jaw that would make one suspect Habsburg lineage, except that it gives her a quality absent in the monarchical dynasty. I think it gives her a countenance exuding confidence, if not control, something no Habsburg could pretend once his portrait was in circulation. Underscoring her button of a nose, the forceful chin imperatively strengthens rather than diminishes her beauty. No, definitely not a Habsburg.

In any case, I was not up to seeing her commanding face peering in at me through a dusty, unkempt window glass in the wee hours of an October morn. I'd had my fill of her these past few months, starting with the first day of class, and I had decided to withdraw my feigned friendship, get out from underneath her threatening chin, and breathe a little. Yet there she was, knocking and calling out my name with no concern for neighbors.

It is true that the nearest neighbor in my village lives a good hundred yards distant, but you have to have heard Cambria's larynx fully exerting itself to appreciate my concern.

"Professor Telsmith!" she hollered, "open up!" A pause ensued so that she could hear her voice echo down through all seven hills of Brownville. "Professor Tristan Telsmith! Open up!" Another pause. "I can see you in there. Get out of bed and open up!" She pressed her chin and nose up against my window and let her eyes wander about my private quarters. "You can make your bed later. And why are your clothes on the floor?"

Propping myself up in bed, I glared at her. She looked somewhat surreal, her shadowy face haloed about by the rising sun behind her, all that could be seen in the flesh was the tip of her nose and chin. I knew I couldn't stare at her hard enough to make her bow her head humbly and slink away; so, beaten, I slung my legs over the side of the bed, grabbed my robe off the floor, stumbled into my slippers, and dragged myself to the front door. When I opened it, there she was as if she'd magically transported herself from the window to my doorstep in an instant.

"Professor Telsmith, is Tasia here?"

I was flattered. To think Tasia, who has to be the most widely appreciated female on campus, at least for her physical attributes, would have spent the evening in my company was quite a compliment. "I don't think so," I said slowly, looking at the kitchen area behind me as if she might be in the house.

Cambria peered round me to have a look for herself.

I really do believe that a kitchen tells more about a bachelor than does his bedroom. An unkempt bedroom may indicate that an energetic young man worked late and fell asleep exhausted before he could match trousers and shirts to clothes hangers, as much as it might indicate the habitual slacker. A sparkling kitchen, however, denotes the character of a man during his waking hours. The swept floor, the polished table, the knives affixed to the wall and ordered by size, the emptied dish sink, etc. all give witness to the presence of a conscientious and dutiful gentleman.

"I see Stanley's in town," came an utterance from the protruding chin below me.

She was right. Stanley is my housemate, paying half the rent and utilities and doing most of the work. The only room he doesn't attend to is mine and that's not for want of trying. I caught him just two days after he had moved in, picking up my robe from the bedroom floor. "Stop!" I ordered. "Leave it be. How do you think I'm going to find it in the dark if it's not the first thing my hand lands on when reaching for the floor?" Stanley, who's majoring in sociology, gave a dozen solutions to my rhetorical question, each one designed to improve my overall well-being, but I dismissed them all and a truce was formulated wherein my threshold marked our DMZ.

You wouldn't guess that Stanley was a stickler for propriety. He doesn't sit about in the evening in slippers propped up on an ottoman whilst laying back into the couch with a copy of *Good Housekeeping* between his thick mitts. No, he spends his evenings at the gym working out. I don't know why; I doubt a bicep can ever surpass the diameter of one's head, and both of his have already reached this limit. And he no longer needs the bulk to play middle linebacker for Aspinwall College's River Rats, (the River Rat being our mascot), given that his bum knee has sidelined him. I think it's a force of habit that he just can't shake, much like I would go on reading books, even if I lost my teaching position.

"Yes, he's back," I said slowly, drawing out the phrase as I spotted something. "You know the dishwasher isn't quite shut all the way. That's going to bother him."

"She's gone missing," said Cambria as if the dishwasher meant nothing to her.

"She could have spent the night with someone, knowing her."

"I've already checked with all the likely suspects. I really didn't think she would be with you, but since she's nowhere else I figured maybe she got drunk and confused you with someone else."

"Makes sense," I admitted. "But how come

you're the one running about looking for her? You two aren't especially close, are you, except in the way two boxers might be in a ring?"

"Jennifer came to my room looking for her around six this morning."

"Jennifer?"

"Her roommate. She said Tasia never came back to the dorm after the party last night, even though Franky saw her coming up from the direction of the Bookshire coffee shop about eleven-thirty. I told Jennifer I'd call the professors and then check with you. Why don't you answer your phone?"

"Because it's Saturday morning. And I'd love to carry on this conversation concerning Tasia's whereabouts, but I feel obligated to get back to what I was doing."

She gave me a snooty "Hmpff" before turning on her heels and climbing back into her aged Aveo and driving off.

I turned about myself, after sending the door home with a bang, and proceeded to boil up some coffee before sitting down at the table with a full cup to ponder a bit about Cambria and Tasia, two very different girls.

***

I discovered Tasia and Cambria back in August, when the semester began, in my Western Civilization class. I have some twenty students and pretty much free rein, even though I'm but a lowly adjunct, teaching three courses, if the dean favors me. My total income is pretty much dedicated to paying my way through to my PhD.

"I'm Mr. Tristan Telsmith," I said by way of introduction on the first day. I gave an up-beat description of myself, underscoring how hard I had worked to excel in academia, and leaving out the part about my parents. If I'd told them both my parents were successful lawyers who wouldn't let me, as a ten year old, watch an hour of television come Saturday if I hadn't read three books of their choosing during the week, one in history, one in science, and one in classical literature, the students might have claimed that I owed nothing of my success to my own endeavors. No, I focused on how I was a self-made boy, taking on a paper route when but twelve years of age. It was the only reason my parents would let me out of the study. "Will do him good," said my father, "to have some practical experience." That was my fun time, throwing newspapers at other peoples' front doors.

After recounting the hardships of childhood, I invited the students to introduce themselves one by one. I couldn't help but notice Cambria's demeanor, self-assured, but seemingly pleasant and poised on that first day. First impressions can be deceptive. She had given a short, confident, but self-deprecating autobiography, and it came as no surprise to learn she'd been homeschooled before attending a private high school, Parkfield Christian.

This delighted me. *What a hand-rubbingly fun task I have ahead of me*, I said to myself. *I really ought to get to know this Cambria girl and bring her round to a better understanding of life. After all, such is the vocation of a professor. Opening up young minds so that they might see the world in the right light, that of academia.*

Tasia, on the other hand, gave herself a less subtle review. Hers included her triumphs in tennis, her performance as a madrigal singer, her theatrical career, if high school drama qualifies as a career, and the highlight of her life, her successful debut in a beauty pageant. After going into the details of the contest and how she found it so hard ditching one of the judges who had fallen for her, I reminded the class in general and her in particular that we had but fifty minutes to get through all the introductions, the syllabus, and an amusing exercise for extra credit.

The word "amusing" caught Tasia's attention. She switched course like a beagle crossing a new scent. "Let's do the amusing exercise," she nearly demanded.

I straightened up to my full height which placed me well above my students, considering they were seated, and informed Tasia that due form must be followed and that the syllabus explanation held precedence. She objected, but I held firm, although I must admit that reciting course requirements on the first day seems a pointless exercise, as no student to date has taken heed of my delineation of points and due dates until the week of final exams, and by then it's often too late to bring a sunken grade to the surface. In any case, I successfully hit the syllabus highlights before embarking upon the amusing exercise.

"What I hope to do through this introductory exercise," I said with sufficient verve, "is to show you the problem of dealing with a subject of history known to us through primary sources. How do we know, for example, about Charlemagne?"

My students pondered this question blankly,

as most had no idea what either a primary source or a Charlemagne was, so I explained. "Charlemagne was King of the Franks and later Emperor of the Romans. We wouldn't know much about him personally if it weren't for Einhard, a court biographer, who described Charlemagne's physical characteristics and personality. You might think, 'Well that settles it. Einhard told us exactly what this barbarian emperor looked and acted like.'" I proceeded to quote from Einhard's biography, where the enthusiastic author noted his "fair haired" hero to be "large and strong and of lofty stature" and habitually exhibiting a "face laughing and merry" that was graced with "large and animated eyes." Then, screwing up my own eyes, I asked the class, "But what if others had given descriptions?"

Feeling the uneasy weight of silence, Cambria spoke up. "We would know more."

"Or," I suggested, "we would be confused, and in the end, know less. Let's see what might happen if we were to write up several descriptions of a person. I need a volunteer, someone who doesn't care being written about; and we'll have all the rest of you play the part of Einhard. You'll write down a description of the volunteer and then I'll select a few and read them out loud."

I had learned not to offer myself as a volunteer. I had done it once and discovered that I was "a thin, shorter version of Clark Kent, complete with nerdy glasses, but someone who could never be Superman."

Tasia was up out of her seat in an instant and presented herself at the front of the class. "I'll do it," she said, shifting a chair about to face her classmates as if she were to sit for a royal portrait.

No one objected and all seemed to write enthusiastically. After collecting the students' descriptions, I shuffled through them. Those written in a characteristically male hand had to be edited. Especially the one ending with an odd tagline, "voluptuous, and I know where you live." The ones I did read proved my point. Did she have dark hair or brown hair or was she a brunette? One description highlighted the cute mole on her left cheek, none other mentioned it.

"Very intriguing, your portraits," I commented in the manner of an art critic. "And I trust you'll appreciate the problem of eyewitness reports. One of you has Tasia with dark hair, another, brown. Now imagine if you just described Tasia in this way verbally and that's all. No written account. The person who hears dark may interpret black, and the one who hears brown might think her hair of a light brown or near sandy color. In no time at all, you have two Tasias. One with black hair and another blonde. So, it's important to get back as far as we can to the original primary source. If we can't, we must be aware that the testimonies we have are probably far from the truth. In this class, you will be history detectives, trying to sort out the original portrait."

***

I found the disparity between Tasia, with a disposition consisting of what a romance novelist might call a bubbly personality, and Cambria, with the cheerfulness of a prosecutor, interesting enough to share with my colleagues at morning coffee, which is ritually held each weekday morning in the chambers of Dr. Henry Langstrom.

"Homeschooled!" exclaimed Langstrom as he leaned back in his brown leather swivel chair, bringing his hands together in order to twiddle his thumbs. He looked up at his bookshelf as if reading off the title of his somewhat well-received work entitled *When Constantine Invented Christ*. "What a delightful challenge."

"I was thinking something of the same sort. Any suggestions?"

The three professors looked at each other encouragingly. The balding professor, Alfred Tate, let out a half-suppressed chuckle, and Professor Simeon, or Sim, Garfield followed suit.

"I had her in a class a year or two back," said Sim, "Introduction to Political Science. Hard to forget the girl. One of those types that sticks to your shoe. If she didn't make some statement condemning abortion once every fifteen minutes, she thought she'd wasted her tuition money. Myself, I thought her existence to be the best argument in favor of abortion."

"Open their eyes and you'll open their hearts," Langstrom said solemnly. He had a heightened interest in opening the minds of students, the blonde female students in particular.

"You should hold a Bible study," he continued, "and get her to attend. I've done that before, very rewarding." He turned to Alfred Tate, our drama professor, and recalled a girl some five years back, (three years before I registered for graduate classes at Kenosha U), who had been won over from the dark side. "She became the life of the party once liberated, didn't she Al?"

"She became the life of everybody's party."

"Listen, Tristan," Langstrom said in what one might call a professorial tone, "tell them you're starting a Bible study on Thursday nights. Tell them you'll give them extra credit for participating. You'll get all your 'A' students to attend, and I'm willing to bet," he continued as he clicked lightly away at his keyboard, "that, being homeschooled and willing to admit it...that she's of that pedigree....." He studied his computer screen. "What's her last name again, Davenport you said? Here she is, nothing but thirties for her ACT scores. Those are the overachievers, the ones who will take on extra credit assignments. God forbid that a footballer two points shy of a D would ever tackle one."

I realize now that my first mistake had been in telling Langstrom about Cambria, my second mistake was following his advice. I should have known better. I remember I had followed his advice once before and ended up regretting it. He had invited me to meet with a group of students one Tuesday night, assuring me that they would be honored by my visit. When I showed up, I discovered I had been ambushed into the local chapter of The Social Sciences Club. I would not have minded except that Langstrom introduced me as their new faculty advisor, a position I've held ever since. I soon noted that I was not just the faculty advisor, I was the only faculty member to attend the meetings, except the annual meeting, when free food is offered. Then Sim, Al, Langstrom, and a host of unknowns show up.

Don't get me wrong, it's not that it's a bad

gig, the students are all fine and as honorable as the society itself, it's just that I'd rather pick up some tacos on Tuesdays and belch away on cheap Mexican beer, while watching an old western or some other Sixties flick. I refuse to suffer alone, however, and I've pretty much made it a requirement that all history majors join the club.

As compensation for my advising duty, Langstrom convinced the dean to allow me to teach an upper level course entitled "The History of Twentieth Century Film." The subject matter is completely out of my line of study, but I love movies and since few students know there were films in the twentieth century, I don't have to know too much to be an expert.

We watch both movies and a selection of episodes from the old TV shows, everything from late twentieth century productions, like *Little House on the Prairie* and *Baywatch*, to old classics, like the 1931 *Dracula*.

I'm not one to point out any possible gender differences in student behavior, but I will admit that few of my male scholar athletes skip out on class on *Baywatch* day. Personally, though, I think Frances Dade, playing Lucy Westenra, even after Count Dracula got his fangs in her, was just as seductive as anyone in a bikini.

However, we mostly analyze westerns: Matt Dillon, John Wayne, Clint Eastwood and the like. There's nothing like a western to confuse a student's mind about values back in the old days. Just think of Dodge City, where the two most upstanding citizens were the U.S. Marshal and the local madame.

***

On the third Thursday of the semester, September 10, two days after our monthly Social Sciences Club meeting, I met Cambria and half a dozen other students at the off-campus coffee shop, the Bookshire. The establishment is located just south of campus along Park Avenue. Walking down to it takes you past a park on the left and a few houses to the right. It sits on the left-hand side, just past a quick shop. It's at the edge of town, and beyond it are visible a dirt road and corn and soybean fields hemmed in by tree-lines and patches of timber.

This shop itself is actually both a coffee and tea shop. Upon entering, you face a counter, with the coffee shop part off to the left and the tea shop on the right. After getting my drink, I went into the coffee shop side, with its window facing counter and booths, and then maneuvered toward the back where there was a room designed for small group gatherings.

Cambria arrived while the rest of us, cups in hand, were sitting down. She sat opposite me at the far end of the table, as if we were the quarrelsome husband and wife keeping a safe distance from each other during meals, for the children's sake.

"I'm surprised you do a Bible study," she said accusatively. "I don't take you for being the religious type."

"Oh, religion, well it's useful, as Karl Marx once noted. It keeps the rabble in place. However, having the advantage of hindsight, I would not line up with Marx today. A dictatorship keeps the rabble in place even better, considering the achievements of Hitler, Stalin, Mao, and Pol Pot. And then there's nothing passive about religion either. Not much of an opiate I'm afraid. I mean look at Martin Luther King, Jr., you can't say his religion kept the rabble in check."

"Religion's still a crutch," said Quinton. "Give it another twenty years and there won't be any more men toting around Bibles and believing in them. Come on, the world created six thousand years ago?"

"I take it you've never actually read the

Bible," responded Cambria. "You've just been fed bits and pieces that have been taken out of context to build a straw man to knock down. Well, believe me, the straw man will get knocked down, but the Bible man will still be standing."

Tasia darted her eyes at me. "I always wanted to know a Bible man." She said this with a voice more attuned to a speakeasy singer than a religious aspirant.

I believe I stuttered after her confession. "I, I would like to be clear that I'm not a minister or anything of the sort. We're here to study the Bible in a purely academic way, from a secular and scientific point of view."

There was a silence while I looked over my collection of students. I noted the Bible study had not just drawn in my A students.

"I take it," Cambria said disapprovingly, "you're going to skip the opening prayer,".

"Oh, by all accounts, pray if you wish," I said thumping the Bible like a good Baptist, "but please do it before coming. As it says in here somewhere, 'Pray in your bedroom', or some such, 'but not out in public.'"

"Closet, according to King James," said Cambria.

"I prefer the bedroom," rejoined Tasia, with

her large eyes and gaping cleavage. Had this been catechism at Rome I would have feared for the salvation of the pope. I, myself, found it hard to resist focusing on the hypnotic ruby gem dangling at the nether end of her necklace.

"Bedroom," I reiterated, with my neck giving the brain a quick shake to break the spell and forcing both eyes and brain to study her eyebrows. I couldn't quite bring myself to face off with her eye to eye, for fear she might see into my soul. "No," I said rather mechanically, "we probably should go with Cambria's suggestion."

The good thing about having an unofficial Bible study is that it typically draws students like Cambria who possess a homespun rather than an academic knowledge of the gospels. Tasia, apparently, had no knowledge either way, but I sensed I could depend on Cambria and some of the others to answer my leading questions.

"Anyhow," I proceeded, "whether from the bedroom or closet, let's take a look at the Bible and see what the New Testament has to say about Jesus." I gave a general overview of the Christian religion, explaining that we even set our calendar by Jesus' birth, whether we denominate it AD, the Year of the Lord, or CE,

Common Era. "Yes," I concluded, "Jesus' birthday generally marks, within a half-dozen years, ground zero."

"So he was born when?" Tasia asked innocently, opening a tiny purse to extract a little pocket mirror that she popped open to review the status of her makeup.

Looking at the little purse, I could hear my mother's voice in the background: "A woman with a small purse has a brain to match."

"Let's say the year zero," I replied kindly. "Now, what we want to know is if we can trust the New Testament documents that tell us what we know about Jesus. Think about it: Do we even know if Jesus really said what's put in his mouth in the gospels?"

"Like about his birthday?" suggested Tasia. "When was it again?"

"Around the year zero, but that's not what I'm talking about. Think about Jesus making a prophecy, for example. Pick one, if you will."

As expected, Cambria provided the quick response. "Jesus' prophecy that Jerusalem and its Temple would be destroyed. He prophesied it would happen, and then it did."

"Well spotted," I said, trying to sound English and therefore cultured. "To think that someone could predict some forty years out the sacking of Jerusalem and the destruction of the Jewish Temple is stretching it, isn't it? Last week I predicted our football team would win Saturday's game, after all, we were favored. As a prophet, though, I'm down five dollars. If I have any respect for myself, in my journal that I'm writing as inspiration for my proud descendants, who will no doubt peruse it with interest, I'll record that I predicted a loss for our heroes and that I added one hundred dollars to my bank account."

One of my less illustrious students, Barton by name, who had been lost since the beginning of Bible study in an effort to examine more fully Tasia's necklace, now rejoined us and said, "So if I wanted to predict that Tasia would go to the concert with me over Thanksgiving Break, then I would wait until we went together before making the prediction."

"No," said Tasia. "You can predict right now that I'm going with someone else, besides you wouldn't have enough money to get me a spot in the pit." She looked over at Franky who was thumbing through his well-worn Bible. "Franky will take me, won't you?" Franky didn't say yes or no, but he did stop thumbing through his Bible. "But first, he's taking me down to Stickers for a dinner date tomorrow night, aren't you

Franky?"

Now, if you were to blurt out the word "macho" to me, the last image that would come to my mind would be that of Franky. I don't know what a handsome man looks like, no man really does, but I do recognize a wimpish one. I mean who else nowadays wears a buttoned up checkered shirt with a collar and uses the pocket to house a slim notebook and seventy-two ballpoint pens? If this were the Sixties he'd have a slide rule sticking up out of it too.

Franky couldn't look Tasia in the eye, any more than I could, he just turned sideways, focusing on a spot on the table next to his Bible, and proceeded to play the chameleon by transforming his cheeks from an off-white color to blood red. This was obviously the first he'd heard of the proposal.

"I fear we wander from the topic at hand," I said to save the poor fellow. "The point is that Jesus' prophecy was made after the fact."

"I don't see why," Cambria objected. "Even if we're looking at this as skeptics, it seems perfectly possible that Jesus made the prediction forty years before it happened."

I don't like people contradicting my opening argument because it seems to shake the strength out of all the subsequent ones built upon it. So, I'm afraid I asked, "How could it be perfectly possible?" with a rather mocking sneer at the words "perfectly possible."

"Well, for one thing, there's Barabbas."

"Barabbas?" asked Tasia.

Cambria looked at Tasia with a raised eyebrow, not unlike the raised eyebrow given by Jesus to Judas, when the latter asked to leave the table. "He was a revolutionary," she said. "The Jews were always plotting revolution. The Romans had already destroyed Jerusalem once before. They had obliterated other capital cities, Corinth and Carthage to name two that begin with the letter 'C'. If I were standing in Judea in 30 AD like Jesus, the safest prediction to make would be that some day Jerusalem would be sacked by the Romans."

Her comment unsettled me. It was an argument one might expect from a non-believer except he would never make it, because it undermined something more important: the fact that the gospels were written forty or more years after the crucifixion.

I think I might have been visibly stunned. I could hear the students' voices in the background. Tasia wanted to know more about Barabbas. I remember Cambria saying something to the effect that Barabbas represented herself, a guilty and heinous criminal that Jesus replaced so that she might live.

Finally, I resurfaced, and I heard Cambria say distinctly, "For us Christians, Barabbas is both fact and symbol."

"Yes, yes," I interrupted. "We do understand the symbolism but we cannot accept biblical claims as fact until we analyze them academically, from a scientific point of view; so, for next time, I would like you to read the gospel of Mark and we can take a close look at it. Remember, it's ten points of extra credit, which will boost your grade at the end of the semester."

"Is that all we're doing for tonight?" asked Angela.

"For our first meeting, I think it's sufficient. We're just setting the ground rules, we'll have much more to learn and discuss next time."

I gathered my things and wandered somewhat sheepishly out into the parking lot to my car. Sitting down at the driver's seat, I promised myself that next Thursday I would come fully armed, mace and all, and deliver a solid blow to the enemy. Right on that chin of hers.

Sitting there, I observed Tasia waiting at the

coffee shop door, while most of the other students lingered inside. When Cambria finally exited Tasia immediately joined her. It seemed odd to me at the time and odder yet now. I clicked the key a notch and rolled down my window to eavesdrop.

"You're really into this religious thing, aren't you?" asked Tasia. "You're not doing this just for the extra credit are you? I'm certainly not, I just like to get to know people."

Cambria stopped to answer. "I'm no more religious than the next Christian, Tasia, but you're right, I wasn't looking for extra credit, I thought this might be a real Bible study, even though I had my doubts from what I've heard from Professor Telsmith otherwise. Nevertheless, it's interesting."

"You see that guy," said Tasia, nodding in the direction of Barton who was coming outside. "Not your type at all is he? You should get to know Franky; I think he's more your type. He's quiet, and he brought a Bible tonight."

I couldn't see Cambria's features very well, as she was turned away from me, but I'm sure she bore the deeply furrowed brow. "I'm here for studies, thank-you very much."

"I think he's hot on you."

"Then he's wasting his time."

"You already have a boyfriend?"

"Not that I know of."

"I bet your parents didn't let you date, did they? No offense, it's just that I picture them being super religious."

"Just as religious as I am. And I see no point in dating unless you're planning on marrying the guy you go out with."

"So...you've never had a guy?"

"Listen, Tasia, we barely know each other, and I've got math homework. I'll see you tomorrow in class."

"I understand, but I do think Franky is a good guy, your kind of guy." Having said this, she returned to the coffee shop.

I rolled up my window and started the car. As I pulled forward and turned, I glanced through the storefront window and caught sight of Tasia again, now talking, and at very close range, with Franky. What was she up to? A match maker? I pressed down on the brake and spied. Tasia now held Franky's hand and he looked awfully awkward and embarrassed. She looked very much at ease and with her free hand she toyed with her gemstone.

Franky's face lit up with a quick but quivering smile, as if someone had attached jumper cables to his oversized ears and given him the juice. With an acquiescing nod, he moved past Tasia and out the door. She followed close behind with words of encouragement. "You'll have a great time. I'll make sure. You pick me up at six tomorrow night!"

***

The drive home to Brownville was lonely. The undulating landscape with its yellowed rows of crop ready for harvest can make one either feel at one with nature or very alone. As dusk settled over me, I felt the latter, even when I finally turned off onto 6th Street and climbed the hill. Once cresting it, I got a full view of the village in its fading autumn dress. Not a soul in sight could I see, as I descended and then turned into my driveway.

After entering the house, I decided to console myself with a mug shot of Tennessee honey. I found the bottle in its lair, a blocked off doorway, whose recess had been converted into five or six shelves. The whiskey was on the top shelf, out of reach of toddlers, in case any might wander in.

I poured out my regular dosage for such occasions, set the bottle on the counter, and grabbed a couple of ice cubes from the freezer as additives. As I sat down, Stanley emerged from his bedroom. He picked up the whiskey bottle and returned it to its shelf overlooking the kitchen. He then put himself across from me and asked, "What's bothering?"

I wasn't going to tell Stanley I'd been bested at Bible study, but I did tell him about the odd conversation I'd overheard between Cambria and Tasia, and I tacked on the equally odd interaction between Tasia and Franky.

"Hey," said Stanley. "She's hitting on him. She just wanted to make sure Cambria wasn't interested in him first."

"But it's so unfair. Franky's a nerd. She's just going to use him and mock him like a judge at a beauty contest."

I'm not sure Stanley understood the importance of the beauty contest reference, but he did understand that Franky was a target. "Well then, you make him undesirable." Stanley got up and returned to the refrigerator where he retrieved a zip-locked baggie with something yellowish-white and mushy inside.

"My parents returned from a trip to France last week and bequeathed this to me. Never open it inside a house, it will kill a mouse without ever setting it in a trap."

"What is it?"

"That's a good question, but I think it comes under the general title of *fromage*."

"Cheese?"

"I see you graduate students do indeed learn more than one language. Yes, cheese, but that's a red herring, because cheese in America does not smell of expended baby diapers moldering away in the garbage. This one does."

"And how is this to make Franky undesirable?"

"Via a warm engine."

I was at a loss but intrigued at the same time, so Stanley elaborated. He explained that since Franky would take Tasia into town in his car, my job was to crawl under the vehicle prior to the date and dispose of the fetid article by reaching up from underneath and placing it on the engine. Stanley assured me the odor would waft its way into the nostrils of the occupants and smother any breath of romance. "It's guaranteed to neutralize any love-mobile for no less than one week, unless you're French, because they have immunity."

***

On Friday morning, I set off early for

campus. It's a seven-mile bike ride but southeast Nebraska is beautiful country and there's a level and picturesque bike trail below the bluffs, which snakes alongside the Missouri River from Aspinwall to points north. I figured I could get one or two more bike rides in before winter snows closed the trail.

Once I had parked my bike, I searched out Mac, our security man, and he gave me the license plate number to Franky Trotter's vehicle, a red Honda Ridgeline pickup, not hard to spot amongst all the Fords and Chevys. I approached it slowly, making sure I didn't attract any attention. I circled it as if I were appreciating the statue of Aphrodite *Kallipygos* in the Naples museum. Feeling confident, I knelt down before her and began to shed my backpack to retrieve the bomb.

"Is there something wrong?" came a voice from behind.

I turned and saw the Ridgeline's owner not three paces from me.

"I guess not," I said hesitantly as I leaned down on all fours and inspected the asphalt. "Nope, I guess I was wrong. I thought I saw a big oil leak. Is this your pick-up?"

"Yeah, I was going to put my books away before heading down to Stickers."

"Oh," I tried to sound surprised, "you're going down to eat at Stickers?"

"You're welcome to come with us, Professor Telsmith."

"Am I? Well, I suppose I can, but I can't stay too late as I'll have to bike home while it's light."

"Great. We're all walking down there. I think it's about everyone in the Bible study. It was Tasia's idea."

***

Stickers Sports Bar and Grill is just north of campus, at the northwest corner of the town square, not too far from city hall. It's a red building with white trim, made of the soft red brick produced in this country, back in the Victorian era. The brick's so soft that rain doesn't run down the walls. The bricks just suck it up. You can also write your name in the brick with a pen knife and lovebirds have been immortalizing their initials in the facade of the Stickers building for more than a century.

Otherwise, inside, Stickers is what one might expect to find in a college town: dimly lit with wide-screen TVs all around, and smelling of beer.

Quinton, whom you might recall as one of

my students as well as one of my atheistic Bible study members, called out from across the room when we entered; he had found a semi-circular booth in the corner.

"Hey," Tasia called back, "We brought the professor!" I won a tepid round of applause from my students.

Cambria scooted in first, followed by me, then Tasia. Franky, Quinton, and Angela made up the rest of the crew. I was glad to see Angela; she's conscientious and an active member of our Social Sciences Club.

As I was getting into position, I glanced at all the faces. It was a strange group. Who would imagine that fundamentalists, atheists, and hedonists would all be friends? Franky and Cambria were the only real Bible thumpers. Angela was a level-headed secular rationalist, Tasia a hedonist at best, and Quinton, a would-be Richard Dawkins.

Tasia turned to me once we were settled in and commented. "I thought you'd spend all your non-class hours reading history books."

"Normally," I answered, "but I thought they might have the History Channel on down here."

My students laughed as they ought when their professor attempts humor, and the politeness put everyone in a good mood. The students, except for Cambria who mentioned her parents, shared very little about their family and home life and quite a bit about their high school escapades. I did find Cambria more human. Something about her intrigued me despite her radical beliefs. Perhaps it was her candor, her openness in sharing things that others sought, for whatever reason, to hide. Though Tasia also caught my attention, but perhaps it was because she repeatedly patted my leg when she talked to me. Overall, I was feeling, well, popular, even attractive. And I leaned back as if master of ceremonies with everyone appreciating me.

Then I heard a pop! Then a sound best described as that of a whoopee cushion, and all eyes turned toward me. My backpack, I reasoned thoughtfully, my eyes cast ceilingward.

And then came the rush, the horrific odor of *fromage*.

The next day I awoke in a joyful mood, then the remembrance of Stickers flooded back into my brain and I groaned. Gathering up my clothes from the floor, one piece at a time, I got dressed and padded into the kitchen. The table was wiped down and polished, shining up at me. A brewed pot of coffee scented the air. It was Stanley's heavy, black coffee. It wouldn't do to try and drink it straight.

I went toward the pantry off the west side of the kitchen. There's what one might call a doorway into it, but without a door. The little room houses the refrigerator on the right side and a washing machine and dryer on the left. Straight ahead is the windowed backdoor.

I opened the refrigerator to retrieve some half-and-half but found none. I closed the refrigerator and looked out the backdoor window. There I espied Stanley on all fours. A little bowl was set in the grass before him and he was pouring out the last of the half-and-half into it. I'd seen him go through the ritual several times before. He's after a feral cat that, for whatever reason, he wants to domesticate. His efforts have not been rewarded, but I would say it's rather understandable why a ten-pound feline doesn't trust a man on all-fours who weighs two-hundred and fifty pounds.

I could hear Stanley repeating "Kitty, kitty, kitty," but the artificially high-pitched voice fooled no one. He then altered his strategy and tried to reason with the animal. "Roscoe's downtown, far away, can't find you here. Come on kitty, kitty, kitty."

Roscoe is the village watchdog. It's not clear whom he belongs to as he eats from many different troughs. He does have a preference for cat food, but not especially a preference for cats, except to chase them. He is the bane of Stanley's cat domestication project.

Looking beyond Stanley I could see the grey-striped cat on the rise of ground at the edge of the backyard timber. It sniffed the air like a seasoned sommelier and gave a single lick to the chops. Stanley inched away slowly from the bowl, and the cat moved down the slope and stopped whenever Stanley did. The tango continued until the bowl and cat were just out of arm's reach.

Stanley lowered his voice and tried to sound seductive. "Come on my pretty, I know you'd love to be petted." He shuffled forth and stretched out his right arm, extending his hand.

His fingers came within a centimeter of the kitty's ears.

Behind Stanley came a stirring and rustle of fallen leaves. The cat's ears perked up and then when flat as it emitted a deep growling sound. Stanley looked around in time to notice the blurred image of a canine galloping toward him, or rather the kitty. The cat dashed up into the timber to find refuge in a tall cedar. Stanley shouted at Roscoe, forgot his bum knee, and sent a kick his way. Roscoe dodged the foot and ran into the timber where he stood on his hind legs, scratching at the tree with his front paws and barking with gusto.

I opened the door for Stanley and took the half-and-half carton from him. Shaking it, I confirmed it was empty.

"There's some in that bowl if you need it," Stanley said.

"I doubt you can get rabies by just drinking after a rabid animal," I observed, "but I'm not going to take any chances."

"I don't understand cats," Stanley said. "They're kind of like women. You know that cat would just love to be loved, but no, she's gotta play hard to get."

"You're not making any reference to Angela again, are you?"

"Yeah, man, you got it. She's like that cat."

"You're saying she won't go out and eat with you even if you get down on all fours?" I looked at Stanley, shook my head, and said accusatively, "I don't think you've ever even said 'kitty, kitty, kitty' to her, much less asked her out on a date."

"I'm workin' on it."

"Why? You two have nothing in common."

"Don't you know nothin' with all that studying: Opposites attract." I could tell Stanley was irritated. He always adopted a slight gangsta mode of speech when either frustrated, nervous, or posing.

"Listen," I explained, "you're six-foot three, she's five-foot three. She spends her evenings in the library, you spend yours in the gym. She reads books, you look at the pictures."

"That's not right, I know books. I listen to them on the headphones when I be workin' out. Ask me about the *Tale of Two Cities*."

"Detroit and Chicago?"

"Come on, my man. I don't think so. It's more like two of those cities over in Europe: Paris and London."

"Okay, so you've got one book you can mention to her."

"No, I get through about a book a week. I bet you she does too. She just can't afford the headset, that's all."

"Right."

"Okay, what I'm sayin' is that I know there's things that just link us together. I can just sense it."

"I think you may have something there," I said encouragingly. "You like girls and she's a girl."

"Hey, why don't you help me out here. After

all, I helped you out."

"I've been meaning to talk to you about that. If you want your cheese back, you'll have to pick it up at Stickers. It's with my backpack in the dumpster." Since we broached the topic, I told him of my misadventure. He countered that the ploy worked nonetheless because Tasia hadn't been able to spin her web around Franky.

Stanley lifted my spirits by telling me I would be viewed as one of the gang now, and that would give a boost to my evaluations. Something not to sneer at as an adjunct. He could see a fulltime position for me in the offing. Maybe one day I'd be named Professor of the Year.

After successfully pumping me up, he finished by saying, "So, Tristan, here's what I'd like you to do." I could tell he was in earnest and even feeling confident, because he totally dropped the gangsta vernacular. "You talk to Angela and find out what she likes. I bet you she likes the same things I do."

"Why don't you just walk up to her and ask her what she likes? For example, ask her what she thinks of a nickel-defense."

"Nah, that would just be weird me walkin' up to her out of the blue. But you know her. She's in your class." He stood there looking at me with cow eyes until he figured he'd convinced me. "And find out what she thinks of me. And then say somethin' good, like 'Stanley loves classical music.'"

"Like Ludacris van Beethoven?"

"See, you've got a gift for words. Just go talk to her for me."

"Like *Cyrano de Bergerac*?"

"That's right, but you don't have to put on the funny nose."

His last comment won me over. To be honest, I knew Stanley wasn't the uncultured athlete he pretended to be, but it did impress me that he had taken to listening to classics like *Cyrano de Bergerac*.

***

Class on Monday was difficult. It's all up to the professor to maintain order through respect, so that an academic atmosphere might hover about the heads of the student body and inspire young scholars to ponder deep thoughts and offer up penetrating critiques. Look at Socrates, he overawed his students through his integrity and serious state of mind, though at home, his wife caused him nothing but trouble. Why, you ask? Because she saw him at his worst, smelling of cheese.

Of course, Socrates looked at his marital situation philosophically. Reasoning that marrying a difficult woman had sharpened his own wit. But it's hard to imagine him keeping a clear mind and discoursing upon his method with Plato chuckling and carrying on in the back row.

For me, after Friday evening's fiasco, generating a healthy atmosphere seemed rather like trying to convince Romulus's she-wolf that she's actually a lap dog. Everyone in the classroom either snickered or waved his hand in front of his nose as I entered. Except Terrance Favorly. At least I thought it was Terrance by a process of elimination. Every other pupil's face was present and accounted for. Terrance's slot in the classroom seating chart was occupied by a face donning a full-fledged, rubberized, military gas mask. The galling thing was that Terrance hadn't even been present for "Fromage Friday" at Stickers Sports Bar. Apparently, word about my backpack's indiscretion had gotten around campus more swiftly than anyone could say "cheese."

I don't know why the students thought this so much fun. After all, on that fateful night I had given evidence that it was just a malodorous misunderstanding. When they were streaming away from the table, I had held up the baggie and shaken it in their general direction to allay their fears, but that only made them accelerate their departure.

Except for Franky. He proved faithful. He waited for me outside, and I showed him the evidence close up. He staggered and I put the bag back in my backpack.

Putting a finger and a thumb to his nose he asked me why I would carry around such a thing.

"I found it in my fridge," I said, "it's something Stanley, who has plainly forgotten our nation's health and safety codes, stashed away behind the milk, probably with the intent of using it to play a prank upon someone. I could see him wanting to put it on some poor sap's engine just for the fun of it.

"I, of course, am no prankster. The last thing you'll catch me watching on YouTube is one of those Japanese shows where a young lady enters into a beachside outhouse whose walls unexpectedly fall away from the toilet."

Franky did raise his eyebrows, but I followed through with my defense.

"No, being averse to shenanigans, I at once, deducing what Stanley might be up to, removed the article from the fridge, put it in my backpack and cycled all the way to campus where I hoped to dispose of it far away from the troublemaker. Remove the gun from the criminal, and all you've got left is a law-abiding citizen. That's my motto. Regrettably, I was distracted from the task by your invitation to Stickers."

I believe I convinced Franky, but I could see on Monday morn that he had utterly failed to have had a positive impact upon his hand-waving classmates.

Being a man of decision, at least when my job is on the line, I decided to bring order to the classroom by a tried and true method: The pop quiz. Of course, the issuing of a pop quiz is nowhere to be found in my syllabus, but fortunately no student to date, as I have intimated elsewhere, has bothered to scan, much less scrutinize, the document. The unexpected examination sobered everyone up instantaneously, which allowed me afterward to wax and wane about Romulus and his she-wolf for a full forty minutes.

I caught Angela before she could exit the classroom and asked her to stay behind a moment. Once everyone was gone, I closed the door to question her.

This was really the first time I got a really good look at the girl. I could see what Stanley found interesting in her. She looked to me to be the type of librarian you'd see in the old black and whites. Her hair up in a bun and her eyes encased in thickly framed glasses. An ordinary, plain girl with no personality. But let down her hair, remove the glasses, put a touch of rouge on the cheeks, and say something funny to make her smile and reveal a full set of white ivories and she's a stunner.

"Well," I said with no game plan in mind. "I've been wondering about you, and ugh, well, I thought since you're our Social Sciences Club scholar, I ought to know a bit more."

Her often downcast eyes looked up at me. It's not like she raised her chin to square off with me. No, it was that timid, head down, eyes up, look.

"Really?"

"Yes," I said, strengthening the voice. "Umm, by the way, do you like sports?"

"I don't know. I've never been to a sporting event."

"Well, all right. We'll say that's a no."

We looked at each other for a moment

before another thought came to mind.

"Umm.... Have any pets?"

"Yes, I have a kitten."

"You do!" I exclaimed. "Very good. So, you like cats, do you? Fantastic."

"Do you like cats?"

"Oh, yes. I guess I like animals in general."

"Do you?" she asked gleefully. "I'm very much the animal lover. I belong to the local chapter of Kindness to Animals. I just think it's horrible the way some people treat animals, locking them up all day. Housetraining them by beating them or throwing things at them if they don't measure up. It's awful, isn't it?"

"I can't agree more. If they taught children that way, they'd lose their rights as parents, wouldn't they?"

"That's the only thing I can get motivated about politically, I suppose, but politics in general just makes me nauseous. People arguing all the time. But I will sign petitions and collect signatures for legislation to protect animals."

"Well, I understand you perfectly. There're just some things one must have convictions about. Take my roommate, Stanley, he's just smitten by classical music. I don't know why. For my part, I can listen to it for a bit, but give me old country western any day. Stanley, though, it's all Beethoven and Mozart."

She smiled as I spoke about Stanley.

"I understand you perfectly as well," she said. "It's true, classical music is fine, but country has a story to tell. Just think of 'From the Ground Up,' it's such a beautiful depiction of love, it's both sentimental and profound."

She took her glasses off and looked me in the eye. "Professor Telsmith, I think you have wonderful lectures. Don't let people like Terrance get the best of you. He's an ass."

"Oh," I said, "well, I'm not nearly as wonderful as you might think. Now take my roommate Stanley, he's someone to admire."

"And that's something I think is so unique in you as a professor," she countered, as she opened the door to leave. "You're not like Dr. Langstrom or Dr. Tate. They're fine scholars, I know, but you're every bit as bright and yet you have humility."

"Oh, no," I said. "I'm the least humble of all."

"There you go again," she laughed.

***

Arriving at the house that Monday evening, I found Stanley waiting at the front door.

As soon as I walked in, he fired off the predictable question: "So, what does she like?"

"Angela? Well, she doesn't like sports," I said on my way to my room to shed my new backpack.

"That'll work, with my banged-up knee, I can't play anyway. So what else?"

"She doesn't like politics."

"No, man, tell me what she does like."

"Okay, she's crazy about animals. Has a cat."

"Wow! We're like made for each other. I

knew it! I've got a cat too. Well, almost. Give me a day or two."

Having deposited my backpack, I plopped down at the kitchen table with my give-me-a-whiskey look. The cheese fiasco had left a stench in my nostrils that kept refreshing the memory and depressing me.

As usual, Stanley coaxed me into telling him about my concerns while not only handing me my Tennessee medicine but also while preparing one of his top chef omelets.

"I remember," said Stanley as he stirred in the eggs, "when Coach wanted to build comradery amongst us players, he'd take us to the pizza parlor. When he wanted to have a relaxed but serious moment with us, he'd invite us over to his house."

I was skeptical and said so. Meeting students outside the classroom and off campus in a neutral setting gave them a certain uppityness that trumped scholarly expertise. Anything I would say would be countered by arguments based upon the authority of the latest Wikipedia edit.

"No, no," he insisted. "You don't get it. Meeting them at the Bookshire is the neutral setting. That's the same as when we'd be at the pizza parlor, when everybody'd get a bit rowdy, but sipping soft drinks in his home, sitting on his plush, cushioned white sofa, being careful not to spill a drop, tamed us all down and made us all ears. We listened to him then."

It made sense.

The result of Stanley's revelation, of course, was that on Wednesday, I announced in class, to those concerned, that the Bible study group would meet on the morrow at my house at 215 South 6th Street, Brownville.

***

On Thursday evening, I arrived home on my bike. As I leaned it up against the south side of the house and took my helmet off, I heard the distinct but unusually high-pitched voice of my roommate, repeating the word "kitty" over and over. Behind me pulled in two carloads of students, some got out armed with Bibles.

"So, this is where you live." Angela commented. "It looks so Victorian. All brick and tall windows."

"Stands to reason," I explained. "It was built in 1884 by Mr. Isaac Nace."

"Wow, Brownville must have been booming back then."

"Well, the year he had it built yes, but the next year the county seat moved to Auburn and that was the final nail in the coffin for the budding metropolis, nobody wanted to be buried with the town, so nearly everyone fled."

"Well," commented Cambria, "I think it was a blessing. The old village retained its soul. It didn't get flattened and buried by skyscrapers. It's rather idyllic."

We stood there atop the hill of the Nace House. Across the street, catty-corner, stood a charming abode, the former residence of Governor Furnas, one of the town's founders. Beyond it, barely visible, given the trees, was the old Methodist church that briefly served as a medical school once upon a time. In clear view, to the northeast, we looked down over the peaceful settlement, quaint and picturesque.

Then a slew of curse words rose up from behind the house, and from around the corner came charging directly at us a rough looking mongrel of a dog at high speed.

He was followed by a battle cry: "Roscoe, I'll kill you!"

"Whoa!" said I. "Stanley! Stop!"

Stanley put on the brakes in front of us, his eyes burning, his chest heaving, and his hand grasping a brick so hard it began to crumble. He looked down upon all of us and then spotted a horrified Angela.

He stood motionless for a moment. Then looked off toward the road where Roscoe had stopped.

"Okay!" I shouted at Roscoe. "One more time! But this is it, because Stanley can't play with you all day!"

Stanley glanced at me and then back at the dog, then at Angela and then back at Roscoe.

"Yeah!" Stanley hollered at Roscoe. "Last time!" He then took the brick and heaved it, and Roscoe watched it sail far over his head and beyond and through Governor Furnas's west-facing window.

Another moment of silence followed, with

Stanley staring blankly at the window.

"Now fetch!" I hollered.

Roscoe ignored me and lumbered off down the street to safer hunting grounds.

Stanley turned toward us, and being nervous, slipped into his gangsta voice. "Oh, my God. Yo' wouldn't believe how much he love ta play fetch. I'm so glad the dude be finally tuckered out. Now," he said to change the subject, "how would yo' like to come in n' listen to some country?"

"Umm, Stanley, they're here for a Bible Study," I said.

Stanley looked at me vacantly, then his eyes shifted to Angela and back to me. "Do I like Bible studies?"

"Well," I suggested, "I did think you wanted to sit in on this one tonight, simply because you like the study of books in general."

"Oh, yes, I listen to more pages than I could ever read."

4

Our little group gathered in the parlor where we had two couches, set in an L-shape, one backed into the recess of the east bay window and the other against the north wall. Opposite the latter I had placed an easy chair from which I intended to direct the Bible study. To my left were three oaken chairs taken from the kitchen.

To be truthful, I was at first surprised to see that not only all the original Bible study students had come, but there were two new members as well. Somehow, my notoriety had made me something of a popular item, like the faded, ripped jeans that a girl buys new off the rack in a high-end store.

In addition, I think there was just a plain curiosity on the part of students, certainly on the part of Cambria, to see what the digs of a professor looked like.

My suspicion is based upon the fact that

Cambria showed none of the politeness and respectfulness of Stanley's teammates at Coach's house. Rather than come into the parlor, gaze about quickly and say, "What a wonderful home you have," before sitting quietly on the couch with hands folded in the lap, she walked the length of the kitchen, then asked, "It looks like you have someone come in to clean, do you?"

"Not officially, no."

"What's in here?" she enquired, looking at the short hallway off the south side of the kitchen.

"Bedrooms. Mine and Stanley's."

She stepped into the hallway and opened the door and stood at the threshold of my inner sanctum. I moved quickly to shut the door but before I could, she asked, pointing at a helpless pair of trousers, "Why are these things on the floor?" I picked them up and stuffed them in a drawer and closed the door so I wouldn't have to find a new home for the socks, jocks, T-shirts, and other paraphernalia.

"If you don't mind!" I scolded, with whatever authority a bachelor might possess.

"You would feel better about your day if you started with a clean room," she pontificated as she opened Stanley's door.

"Ah," she said. "I see who the maid is."

I herded her out of Stanley's room and back into the parlor where the others, along with Stanley, awaited like obedient football players.

I began the Bible study with a general run down of Judaism, because the first Christians were, of course, all Jews. Better Jews, if you had asked them, than all their circumcised brethren, priests included, who had rejected Jesus, their version of the Jewish Messiah.

Now that Cambria had settled down, I noted that there was a certain wisdom in Stanley's recommendation. The students did appear somehow different to me. Sitting up straight, properly, inclining their heads politely.

This encouraged me, so I continued on about how the Jews, whether Jesus followers or not, were very akin in thought and behavior to the rest of the men and lady folk huddled about the Mediterranean under Roman auspices. They all, whether Jew or Gentile, slave or free, believed in the supernatural, in angels, demons, and miracles.

I was on a roll.

"No doubt these beliefs made a physician's job ever the easier, and cheaper," I said with the appropriate note of professorial irony in my voice. "No need to invest in a stethoscope and thermometer. 'Why,' I can hear the good doctor say, 'it's the demon Abaddon at work in your boy; so pray the following seven times a day while standing in the household doorway: 'Begone bothersome Abaddon in the name of the One Most Holy!' and the demon, though perhaps making your child foam at the mouth for a minute or two, just to show off, leaves your little boy as right as rain...if, of course, you first make a voluntary donation amounting to one drachma.'"

Tasia wanted to know what a drachma was, and once I told her it was a coin equal to a day's wage, she suggested a cheaper way of paying off the doctor.

"I'm sure that happened," I opined, "but the real point is that the way people looked at the world back then, whether Jews or pagans, was very much the same. One religion doesn't really differ in its fundamentals from another."

Cambria, having never played football, lacked the self-discipline of Stanley and his teammates at coach's house and objected stridently.

"Hogwash!" she said. "The God of the Jews had nothing in common with the gods of the pagans! Saying that Judaism and paganism were basically the same because they were both religions is like saying capitalism and communism are exactly the same because they are both economic systems."

"No," I countered, "what I am saying is that the Jews and Gentiles alike believed in supernatural happenings, just like you and I both believe in bacteria and viruses."

She went silent for a moment, then asked, "You don't believe a supernatural thing can happen?"

By now I had learned to be leery of Cambria's seemingly innocent questions. And in this case, her tone reminded me of that of my mother's when she woke me up at six a.m. one Saturday morning and asked me, with equal innocence, if I had bumped into anything with the car. My instinct, which I had no reason to doubt that early in the morning, was to say "No." Instinct did not serve me well, because Mother had inspected the vehicle at five fifty-five a.m. and duly noted that the front bumper had acquired, in the night whilst I was out joyriding with my friends, definite V and U-shaped creases across the front of it, creases equal in breadth and shape to what one might expect to find associated with posts implanted in the ground to uphold mailboxes.

I responded carefully, even kindly, to

Cambria. "I didn't say that, albeit I've never seen anything supernatural happen myself, except for my passing calculus back in the day. That exception aside, we're going to have to look at the Bible without inserting supernatural explanations for the events described in it. We'll approach it in a scientific manner, a secular manner, meaning that we can only look at facts, at things that actually could happen according to the laws of science." I felt like I was being a little redundant, but it is true, as even Hitler recognized, that if you repeat something often enough, people start taking it for granted as true. So, if Hitler could do this by repeating nonsense, I certainly should be able to achieve the same end by repeating things that were absolutely true.

Cambria shook her head. "So, you're starting with the premise that supernatural things can't happen and then you come up with a conclusion that supernatural things didn't happen."

Tasia, who sat beside me, laid her hand upon my forearm. "This is confusing. Can we just listen to what Professor Telsmith is teaching us?"

I looked at Tasia's hand upon my arm. It's like she was transferring energy to me because I felt a warmth underneath her hand that spread throughout my body. She smiled ever so slightly at me as if she knew what was transpiring within. Her dark, soft eyes reached into my own, putting me into a near trance. I looked away at the others. They all seemed to be ignorant of Tasia's effect upon me. All, perhaps, except Angela, who seemed to study us.

"If we're going to let miracles into our world of cause and effect," I said shaking off the spell, "then nothing will be certain; we'll never know if something happened for a reason or not. If we want to look at things in that way, then we go to church, but if we want to look at things differently, as in accordance with the way we live our daily lives, minute by minute, as if every effect has its cause, then we study it in a scientific fashion outside of church, and since I see no pulpit, I'll assume we're not in church."

I half expected Cambria to come out of her seat, slap me, and then march out of the parlor and barricade herself in Stanley's room. She didn't. She just sat back in her chair with her arms crossed and said, "Amuse me then."

I wish she'd said something else because I found no comeback to such a cryptic imperative, but it did bring a halt to her caustic interventions. I was able to continue my explanation of the ancient world and how the biblical stories about Jesus came to find their way into what we now call the New Testament.

"The first Christians," I explained, "could only pass on the Jesus tales by word of mouth because they lived in an oral culture: Very few people could read or write. I'm not saying it was a world of toddlers, albeit it might have been better taking advice for an ailment from your two-year old than from the seventy-year-old physician Galen, who would reduce your fever by draining your blood.

"No, it wasn't until the Industrial Revolution and the advent of public education that commoners would become literate. So, this is why the Jesus tales were communicated from one person to the next by word of mouth, until finally, when the movement became larger, forty or fifty years after the crucifixion, after Jesus' first followers had died, some scribes, no doubt worrying that the tales would be lost, took pains to write down the latest renditions of Jesus' doings."

Franky studied me and through his eyes I could see a dim light beginning to brighten his mind.

***

The next day, I was in the cafeteria with my fellow "Miscreants" eating a salad. Angela happened by and paused to say hello.

"You got the Caesar salad, I see," she observed. "Looks good, it's exactly what I was thinking of having."

"Right," I said. "You can't beat Caesar."

"Oh, you're so funny, Professor Telsmith. It was such fun at your house last night, I hope I...or we, get to come over again...for Bible study, of course."

"David and Bathsheba, you're studying?" asked Sim.

"Well," said Angela, "I'm not familiar with them, but we were talking about the New Testament in general."

I really didn't have the appetite for discussing the origin of the Bible, so I was rather pleased to see Tasia join us. "Oh, Tristan," she said, "I just wanted to tell you what fun I had last night. And that roommate of yours and his dog. What a riot. And that little village you live in, how awesome. Is that house across the way, the one with the broken window, for rent?"

"That would be the Governor Furnas Museum," I said. "I don't believe so."

By this time, Tasia had somehow managed

to eclipse Angela who stood behind her like the fifth wheel to a wagon. I didn't mind, it was hard to focus on anything else as Tasia leaned over toward me and carried on. I have no remembrance of what she said, but I did notice Angela slipping away over to the jukebox where Stanley was. I soon expected to hear the twang of country music drifting toward us.

Once Tasia put her hand on my back and gave me a little massage before leaving, I got a better picture of the jukebox couple. Stanley hadn't neglected to adjust the music to Angela's taste, and he was obviously excited to be in her presence. I don't know what he was saying, but he was saying a lot of it.

Angela's reaction was strange. At one moment she seemed to be engaged with Stanley and laughing away, then at the next moment she would look over in my direction with a serious and intense gaze, but just for a fraction of a second. Then back to Stanley with giggles.

"That was Angela, The Social Sciences Club girl, wasn't it?" asked Al.

"The first girl, yes," I answered.

"I wasn't sure. I've only seen her wearing glasses."

"Yeah," I said, only then realizing she hadn't been wearing them. "I suppose she has contacts too."

"Apparently a pretty big contact," said Sim, gesturing in the direction of Stanley.

"Yes," I agreed. "It looks promising."

***

When Stanley came home later that evening, he was fairly proud of himself. He and Angela had hit it off and she was expected to dinner Saturday night.

On that Saturday afternoon, while I sat in the living room and watched John Wayne spank Maureen O'Hara in *McLintock!*, Stanley spent the afternoon scrubbing and polishing our already clean and shiny furniture.

"You know," he said as he lifted my feet off the coffee table and dusted underneath them, "a sensible girl always judges a man by the cleanliness of his quarters and by how he treats his mother."

Stanley had obviously slipped into one of his philosophical moods. I rather appreciate it when he does, because he drops the gangsta talk completely.

I suppose I ought to give you a fuller description of Stanley, since he and I have been crossing paths for some time now. For starters, I will say that Stanley is an all-round good person. In high school I was friends with his brother, Travis, who is my age, but Stanley, being only three years younger, often participated in our escapades. And it's true he treats his mother well. It was she who inspired him to keep house and take up cooking. She even wrote his name on the dustpan and vacuum cleaner and gave him ownership of one of her aprons embroidered with flowers. She rewarded him for dusting and polishing and fixing dinner by letting him go down to the school playground in the evening to play baseball, football, or whatever sport the season offered. Stanley's brother was not the athletic type, so it was hard for their mother to bribe him into much of anything. This meant that when I was free, I went over to their house to hang out with Travis, and perhaps play a video game, because such entertainment was hard to come by in my own home.

In the end, I would say any girl who latched onto Stanley couldn't go wrong if she imagined married life devoid of cooking and cleaning duties.

Angela arrived around six and by this time Stanley was in the midst of concocting some type of vegetarian stew, a ratatouille, he called it. He also had a bowl of rice ticking away in the microwave and bread baking in the oven.

When she knocked, he hurried to the door and opened it. I rather wish I could have seen her expression. It's not often that a door opens to a six-foot-three chef of 250 pounds wearing a flowered apron made for a short and slender woman. As far as I could tell, if she had the inspiration for a burst of laughter, she proved master of her emotions.

Stanley, being the consummate chef, introduced her to our kitchen and then proceeded to share his culinary knowledge with her for some thirty minutes before turning off stove and range and delivering the goods to the table. I admit it all smelled wonderful, but when I heard them sitting down I left the living room, which has no door separating it from the kitchen, and wandered through the kitchen and then into the pantry to grab a drink from the fridge before retreating to my bedroom, so that the lovebirds might enjoy a nest of their own.

Once in my happy place, surrounded by books on the walls and clothes on the floor, I put my tall, cold beer next to my rocker, donned a headset, cranked up the music enough to mask their voices with the ambiance of instrumental music, "Tear Drops on My Guitar," to be precise, and began reading about hermits. After a near hour of reading, I had need to rid myself of the beer. I took off the headset and opened the bedroom door. Stanley by now was discoursing on the variety of desserts and why he had picked the one he did, apple pie a la mode.

"The apple is the best of fall fruits, and the Red Delicious, at this moment, has just the right dark color, so I bought a sack full at Kennedy Orchard. You might think a Granny Smith would outclass the Red Delicious, on account of the green apple's tartness, but there's something about the local climate that gives the Red Delicious a perfumed apple flavor that's not too rich. To make the pie, however, a homemade crust—"

"Oh," I said, "sorry to interrupt, but the call of the wild, or is it of nature, can be heard."

"Yeah, man, no prob," said Stanley. "We were just going to sit outside a bit and listen to the birds and all. You gotta admit, this village is really like living in the country. A haven for animal lovers."

"You'll come out too, won't you?" Angela asked me.

"Oh, no," I said. "Birds tend to frighten me."

"No, man," said Stanley, hoping to please

Angela, "it's cool, you come on out."

After I had done my duty and Stanley had cleared and scrubbed the table, we settled into the lawn chairs behind the house where none of the neighbors can pry. The conversation was lagging as I think we had exhausted Stanley's recipe book.

I decided to discuss animals, knowing Angela's affinity for them. The topic prompted Angela to ask Stanley about his cat.

"Oh, yeah," he said, slipping back into his vernacular as he always did when nervous. "Umm, Psycho, yeah, she's around here somewheres. I let her run 'cause you don't wanna take the freedom from a cat."

"What kind of cat is it?"

"It's your regular grey cat, you know, with stripes, except on its tail. Its tail is all grey but with a white tip at the end of it."

"Is that it at the edge of the timber there? It looks just like you described it."

Stanley and I glanced toward the timber and sure enough there sat Psycho.

"Oh, yeah," Stanley acknowledged. "That be Psycho, just chillin'."

"Could you bring her here?" pleaded Angela. "She's so cute."

"Yeah, no problem," said Stanley.

I noticed a hesitation in this response of his.

"Of course," Stanley added, rising ever so slowly from his lawn chair. "She and I have dis lil' game where she scamper into da timber. She do it so as I have to go find her. It's kinda cute."

As Stanley walked toward Psycho, somewhat like a bushman approaches prey, I noticed I wasn't breathing. It was like watching a movie where someone is dropped into the water with clamps about the ankles and chains attached to the clamps on one end and to a four-hundred-pound concrete block at the other. There goes the poor sap, sinking ever deeper, the bubbles issuing from the nostrils, the hands frantically digging into the pockets. Out comes a penknife, and the desperate man inserts it into a keyhole in the clamp. He turns the knife left and right. And there you are, in front of the screen, holding your breath, and fifteen minutes go by and the sinking man has only one of the clamps off and you're passed out on the floor.

So, you can understand that I, leaning forward in my lawn chair, was urgently hoping Stanley would step on the gas so I could get some air again. But no, he took the long way about. It was a tactical move no doubt. He planned on placing himself between the cat and the timber. Though I was turning blue, I couldn't totally object to his strategy. For some reason, perhaps because he had cut off the escape route or because the giant cat lover wasn't on all fours, Psycho didn't stir. I hoped she was purring.

Finally, after a while, Stanley entered into the three-foot range, and stretching forth his hand slowly, he said "kitty?"

That was the signal. Psycho's fur shot out like she'd been electrocuted, and she bolted straight for us while letting out a low-pitched blood curdling yowl. Angela stood up in horror, I was locked in place by fright and passing out for lack of oxygen. Psycho, seeing no other option, leapt onto my lap. With her sitting there I dared not move. Her eyes were focused on Stanley and Angela and, as I believe Shakespeare once put it, she hissed poignards.

Her claws sunk into my thighs and I exhaled, while wincing and emitting a measured, subdued, and extended "Ahhhhh." Then I took a deep breath and gently slid my hand down the back of the cat. She continued to growl, but the volume diminished as I continued to pet her. Finally, her growls metamorphosed into purrs.

"Huh," said Stanley, forgetting his storyline, "she's never jumped in my lap like that. She always runs away before I can touch her."

"Ohhh," Angela said sweetly, "animals can just sense people who are kind. Professor Telsmith is just a pet-person, that's all."

On Monday morning, September 21, I cycled my way to campus, thinking about how Psycho and I had become fast friends. The cat even cozied up to Angela. Stanley, however, had to social distance at three feet or else she would start digging her claws into whoever held her.

The ride was pleasant, the fall colors making their mark among the cottonwoods and sycamores. Between Brownville and Aspinwall is Nebraska's nuclear plant, parked along the Missouri and protected by tall dikes. Soon thereafter is the mouth of the Little Nemaha. After crossing it over the repurposed railroad bridge, the bike trail keeps flat until Aspinwall itself, and then, after turning south alongside Langdon Bridge, it's a solid pump up the hill toward campus. Once at the college, I left my bike by Neal Hall, where Arts and Sciences is headquartered, entered the building, and strode up the stairs, two at a time, bound for Langstrom's office.

However, I was greeted at the top of the stairs by Sonia Abbot, professor of sociology and general mischief. Despite her being a next-door neighbor to Al Tate, our drama professor, there's something of an on-going battle between her and the cell of Miscreants that meet for coffee each morning in Langstrom's chambers. I do enroll my name among the Miscreants, but mainly because there's no other choice for comradery. Their universal sarcasm is, more often than not, funny, but it is consistently mean-spirited and makes me ill-at-ease, even though I laugh.

As I'm a young newcomer, being only twenty-four, and an adjunct of no standing, meaning an employee who may or may not have a class to teach, depending upon the dean's humor the day classes are assigned, Dr. Abbot, or Sonia as she prefers me to call her, easily engages me. To her peers she systematically gives what might be called short shrift: cold, heartless "hellos," something like Betty Friedan might say when crossing paths with John Wayne after watching a movie of his in which he spanks a grown female.

"Tristan, how are your classes coming?" she

asked lightly. "I noticed a student coming out last week with a gas mask in hand. Are you doing show and tell?"

I almost answered, "More like show and smell," but thought better of it.

"No, Dr. Abbot, uhm, Sonia, I suspect the student is in the National Guard or Reserves and was heading off for drill after class and so brought his gas mask with him."

"And your dissertation on hermits, is that going well too?"

"A lonely topic but coming along nonetheless."

"I'd like to read it when you're finished. It will give me something to go on if anyone should ask me about you when you apply for future jobs. I know so many deans and presidents that I'm sure I can help you along. The last adjunct we had was a disaster and I had to make it known to his would-be employers. I'm so glad he finally decided on a career in hospitality. Waiting tables down at Stickers is such a better fit for him."

"Chris does a fantastic job."

"Yes, doesn't he? Anyway, I might have a little favor to ask of you shortly, so do read your emails." As she said this, I think either a gnat flew into her eye or she intentionally winked at me, one of the two.

Anyway, having encouraged me in reading my emails, she smiled with a nod and moved on with a sway that would win her a place in one of Tasia's beauty pageants, if only they accepted contestants past their best-by date.

Knocking on Langstrom's door as I entered, I was surprised to find one of my Bible study students ensconced in my chair.

"Well hello Professor Telsmith," said a bright-faced Tasia.

"You're up early I see," I replied.

"Yes, no reason to stay in bed, and I wanted to meet with my adviser."

"That would be me," said Langstrom, the only remaining person in the office.

Given that my seat was taken, and the other Miscreants absent, and Langstrom having advising to do, I attempted to escape, but my colleague, if that's not too presumptuous a term for an adjunct to use, insisted I "take possession of Al's seat."

I complied and sat patiently while he gave Tasia the best advice I could imagine, which was to drop her biology class.

After she left, I carried forth about my hermits for a good ten minutes, principally discussing the ministry of Simeon Stylites, best known for having spent thirty-seven years trying to figure out how to get down from a pillar.

When I finished with Simeon, Langstrom asked me about my Bible study. I told him of Cambria's antics, and he, in turn, gave me some good pointers on how to deal with the female fundamentalist. When Al joined us, I got another pointer or two.

I must say that when Langstrom and Al put their heads together their intellect increases exponentially, but only for mischief. It's probably due to the fact that the two of them trod the same high school campus grounds and at the same time. Those who come of age together understand each other like brothers. It's a mutual understanding that never leaves them, even if they haven't seen each other for eons. As soon as they get back together, after a forty-year hiatus, by the second sentence of conversation they're back slapping and giggling at cryptic innuendoes like high schoolers once again.

What makes this especially true for the two Miscreants at hand is that Al Tate and Henry Langstrom never parted ways. Normally "going off to college" splits up devious spirits, but these two attended the same university, and belonged to the same fraternity, and they both worked as liaison officers to local high school history teachers. The two are so close they both drive a late model Lincoln Navigator SUV. So, it stands to reason that when Langstrom landed a job at Aspinwall College, he manipulated the hiring committee into offering a contract to his old classmate. I say this as if it were somehow unethical, but it wasn't, not in the world of academia. Faculty tend to hire their own, at least in terms of ideological preference, and Henry and Al are of one mind politically and philosophically.

Benefitting from their combined suggestions, I felt well-armed for the next biblical encounter with Cambria. I thanked them for it, and both told me I owed them nothing for the consultation except to give them an after actions report once I had brought the young lady to heel.

Finally, Langstrom said he had to call his editor and I took the hint by downing my coffee. I got up, but Al lingered and told Langstrom that he needed to talk to him about the Professor of the Year Award. He had apparently been talking to the chair of the committee responsible for awarding the prize and was not at all happy with what he had heard.

The award was only for fulltime professors, which meant the conversation didn't interest me, so I opened the door.

"Wait a minute," said Al. "You don't have any plans to attend President Larimer's homecoming party on Friday, do you?"

I told him I did not, as the college president didn't even know my name.

"That's great!"

I had no clue as to what was great about having a party without me, but I later discovered it would have been to my benefit to have lingered in Langstrom's office and to have participated in the rest of their conversation. It would have saved me a load of trouble.

***

My next move was to the adjuncts' office. Five of us from various disciplines occupy a room that could easily provide enough space for two real professors.

As I am the last adjunct hired, my desk faces the door, which makes me the gatekeeper. I had been sitting at my post for some twenty minutes, preparing for my next class, when Tasia appeared at the door.

"Professor Telsmith," she said, "I'm so sorry

to bother you, but I forgot my laptop in Dr. Langstrom's office and he's not there. Is there any way you can get it for me?"

I told her no one could go in there without his approval, except the janitor, and the only thing he'd be allowed to touch would be the wastebasket, never a laptop. Her nose was pointed down at the floor, but her big, soft, dark eyes reached upward and settled on my own. I could see a sweet smile lifting the corners of her mouth, and admittedly, I was melting under the gaze, but I had no means of satisfying her request, which was, no doubt, to pick the lock to Langstrom's office, hand her the laptop, and then march off to prison aside security officer Mac Clifton.

Realizing her hypnotic powers had failed her, her smile transformed itself into a thoughtful pressing together of the lips. I waited a moment to hear the result.

"That's all right, Professor, I can talk to the janitor, I'm sure he'll help me."

***

Monday's lecture, except for the reaction I got out of Cambria for my closing statement, was rather uneventful, even though we fought through the Peloponnesian Wars, entertained ourselves with Sophocles' *Antigone*, and went deep into Plato's cave. I think there were two things that kept Cambria at bay during all but the tail end of the lecture. First, I don't think she knows as much about the Greeks as she thinks she does about the early Christians. Second, I think she may have agreed with me.

You see, perhaps unlike my fellow Miscreants, I'm willing to admit that the Judeo-Christian culture contributed values that most people in the world, and not just whites, appreciate every day. But that doesn't mean everything the Jews and Christians believed in are either true or worthwhile. Nevertheless, I think it does surprise students, both the fundamentalist types like Cambria and the non-religious types, like Quinton, Tasia, and perhaps most others, that I would give the Christian religion some credit for contributing to certain beliefs and values that modern and even non-religious people, like myself, appreciate.

The first thing I mention that surprises some is that the ancient Jews and the ancient Greeks had a similar understanding of the world, and not just on account of their mutual superstitions. "The Greeks, through their philosophy," I told the class, "and the Jews, through their theology, shared a similar worldview, one that most people identify with today in their daily lives."

Quinton thumbed through the textbook and raised his hand. "It says in our book that the Greeks brought us a secular worldview. The Jews were religious nutters."

"But they both believed there was a Prime Mover who set everything in motion," I explained. "Of course, they reached the same conclusion by coming at it from different directions."

"How so?" asked Cambria, and without hostility.

"Well, the Jews," I said, "started with the idea that a Creator God with a rational and impeccable mind existed."

"Okay, I can go along with that."

"I'm very pleased to have your approval, Miss Davenport."

"Only so far," she said. "What's the rest of the story?"

"I think it's obvious. Based upon their assumption, they therefore believed this imagined deity would have created a rational and moral world."

"Imagined?"

"To me, anyway. They thought he existed."

"Why wouldn't they? He does. And the Greeks?"

Ignoring her little barb, I explained. "Well, the Greeks, on the other hand, first observed the world about them, much like scientists do today. And they could see that the universe was rationally organized and functioning and that human beings possessed a sense of right and wrong. Therefore, ignoring the randomness that scientists now recognize, they concluded that there must be a Prime Mover pushing everything along rationally toward an ultimate Good. It's a nice fantasy, but there's nothing dictating it."

"That's for sure," said Quinton. "Right and wrong is just a code we live by in order to propagate the race. Which means that as long as whatever I do doesn't harm anybody else, I'm really free to do it. It's the religious quacks," he said eyeing Franky, "that started up this idea that alcohol is wrong, marijuana is wrong, sex is wrong, abortion is wrong, fun is wrong, et cetera, et cetera."

"How are you going to propagate the race aborting babies and being gay?" Cambria barked.

"Woah!" I said. "Let's all calm down. People believe different things. And I should add that all ideological systems, whether theological or philosophical, have inconsistencies. In fact, much of the theological and philosophical writing is dedicated to weeding out inconsistencies."

"Like the Book of Esther," said Cambria.

Now it was my turn to ask, "How so?" I was surprised to hear a fundamentalist admit that her Bible, though perhaps the most self-contradictory handbook in the world, had an inconsistency.

"Esther had the choice to either try to save her people and face execution for trying, or not try to save her people and die anyway by the hand of God. In either case, the Jewish God would have saved his people, even if Esther chose the second option. In other words, God, being all-powerful, always possesses an infinite number of ways to get something done if you don't want to do it for him."

"And what's the point?"

"Free will. We have free will, but God works out his will through history all the same. You'd think because he's all powerful, then we'd just be his robots, but it's not so. We always have a choice to do what's right or to do what's wrong. So the Book of Esther solves the apparent inconsistency."

"We're made the way we are by nature," said Tasia, rather aggressively. "It's just your genes, your past, and the cards life deals to you. You get to play the cards, but you're only happy if you get what your genes and your past have determined you'll need."

"I fear," I said, "that we stray from the matter at hand, which is how the Jews and Greeks were not as different as perhaps your textbook suggests." To show how the Greeks tried to make sense out of the visible world using a rational approach, I read through Plato's "Allegory of the Cave."

After I had explained the whole campfire scene in the cave, Cambria couldn't help but say, "Okay, I get it. Both Jews and Greeks used logical arguments. I imagine Buddha did too. So what's the point you're trying to make?"

For once, she had asked a helpful question. I cleared my throat and explained. "I want to stress the similarity between Jewish and Greek understanding, because it will help explain why the Greeks were intellectually attracted to Judaism, and why, once the Christian evangelist Paul said Greeks could become Christians without losing their foreskin, they flooded into the Christian religion: Christianity, like Greek ideologies, provided them with a systematized worldview that was internally logical and yet allowed for superstition.

"Now," I told the class with my concluding sentence, "I'm not saying that Christianity, or any religion for that matter, is logical, at least from a secular or scientific point of view, but religion does appear logical to those who give up reason to follow faith. Class dismissed!"

That, of course, set Cambria aflame. Marching up to me, she made the old claim that faith and reason go hand in hand, and that, and I quote her here verbatim, "any worldview that starts without a creator God has already given up reason to begin with!"

Fortunately, once a professor utters the words "Class dismissed!" There's little chance for a student rebuttal to be heard. The books being shut, the papers being shoved into backpacks, the zippers zippering, the chairs scooting back, the students talking amongst themselves, etc., all proved effective in muting Cambria's outburst.

After class, I lunched with the Miscreants at the cafeteria and was surprised to learn that Tasia had succeeded where none other had.

"She had her way with Janitor Dovich," Langstrom informed our little coven, taking his seat with a platterful of lasagna. "He felt obligated to tell me. I think he felt rather guilty about it. He said he couldn't really refuse her because she'd left her phone in her laptop bag and she'd left her laptop bag in my office. She had told him that she was expecting a call from her grandmother in Michigan, a very sick woman. I told him that he shouldn't have troubled himself because grandparents don't die until finals week. Anyway, he said the girl was adamant and took her phone from her laptop bag, checked it, and said that Grandmother had indeed called. She surprised Dovich by giving him a peck on the cheek and thanking him before walking off. Dovich said her behavior was rather curious."

"I agree," said Sim. "It's a little odd, kissing the janitor. Would have never crossed my mind."

"No," said Langstrom, "Dovich thought it odd because he thought she would have gone into a semi-shock seeing a missed call from her dying grandmother's phone, and that she would have immediately returned the call right then and there."

Our professor of drama, Al, lifted his hand, and with his palm smoothing down the sparse strands of hair sweeping over his crown, he uttered a soft-spoken "Oh, my." He said this as if playing the part of Miss Marple, where she utters some such quiet exclamation in response to incoming news that makes absolutely no sense to anyone but the sleuth herself.

Langstrom looked at Al and snorted.

It wasn't like a stag snorting at the sight of a challenger, but more like a snort provoked by some distant memory that one would have thought buried and forgotten. "Yes," he said looking at Al, "Patricia was and is a boring, embittered, and yet nastily suspicious one."

"That's putting it mildly," said Al as he

turned to me. "When we were in grad school, his wife, Patricia—"

"Soon to officially be my former wife," interjected Langstrom as he scooped up a spoonful of lasagna.

"Yes, his soon-to-be-former wife convinced the janitor to let her into his office. I came in and found her trying to get into his emails, which were a new thing back then. I think it was to see what women he had been corresponding with." Al winked at me as he lifted his paper cup and sipped soda from a straw.

"Well, one in particular," noted Langstrom. "That freshman drama student you should never have introduced me to. She was bad luck all around. I guess nobody told her to break a leg."

"Yes, bad luck mostly to herself," added Al. "She may have been a one-month stand, but otherwise, as I recall, you would have nothing to do with her. However, it didn't keep her from trying to contact you. How fortunate for you she finally got herself a boyfriend."

"Yes, and he got himself killed in an auto accident, probably trying to escape her," Langstrom theorized.

"She was in the vehicle too, you remember. She got her face mangled up, didn't she?

Couldn't get any acting parts after that." He paused and looked up as if remembering something. Then he chuckled and said, "I think she could have bagged a part in *The Witches*, probably as Grand High Witch."

"I think my Patricia would have been a better choice for that role." As Langstrom said this, his eye caught something in the distance and he made a quick nod of the head toward the far corner of the cafeteria behind me and asked, "Is that your blonde fundamentalist?"

I twisted around and saw Franky seated beside Cambria. It looked as though Franky had a Bible splayed open before him while Cambria typed away at her laptop. What kind of ambush they were plotting for me at Bible study I could only imagine.

My instincts lifted me out of my seat and sent me stealthily across the dining area to spy upon the enemy camp. By coming up from behind I hoped to gather important intelligence; however, they had an observation post set up two tables over in the form of Quinton Harrison, who was pretending to enjoy our chef's latest culinary innovation: mashed potatoes with gravy.

"Hi Professor Telsmith!" he fired off when I came within range.

I thought about visiting with Quinton and explaining to him that he was aiding and abetting the enemy, somewhat like Paul von Hindenburg handing over the chancellorship to Mr. Hitler, but it was too late. Out of the corner of my eye I saw the laptop slam shut.

Cambria said "Hi," but Franky looked at me inquiringly and said, "If they 'passed them on by word of mouth,' wouldn't the stories change a bit?"

I realized he was referring to what I had said at the Bible study about the early Christians passing along Jesus stories from one to another until they were finally gathered and copied down in the gospels.

"Exactly," I responded.

"Nonsense," said Cambria.

"It's not nonsense, Cambria," I riposted, putting my hands flat down on the table and leaning over her for effect, "unless we're going to reject the conclusions of all modern biblical scholars."

"Nonsense," she reiterated, looking aside as if their opinions meant no more than my own. "The consensus rejected Galileo. You should have attended Parkfield Christian High, there are plenty of Galileos teaching there. Anyway, Jews and pagans. Apples and oranges when it comes to literacy. The Jews could have easily jotted down Jesus' words, even while he was talking to them."

I suppressed a guffaw at her bit of malarkey and tried to talk to her as a well-honed psychologist might to an unstable mental patient convicted of strangling to death seven doctors. "They all lived in the same civilization, Cambria, they had the same Roman imperial government over them, lived in the same economy, had the same education, which was none for the most part."

"Not at all," she said standing up and squaring off in front of me with violent intent gleaming in her eyes. I looked down at her hands and she was flexing them, which made me put my own hand to my neck in a justified defensive move.

"For one thing," she spouted off, "the Jews had a completely different religion. For another, their religion was reinforced by a holy book, the Bible. That book helped direct a Jew's entire life, gave him meaning and purpose. The Jews needed to know how to read in order to understand their Bible so they could live the best lives possible. Did the Gentiles have a holy book? No. They had no substantial incentive to learn how to read and write."

"The elite Jews, for sure," I said. "The priests and rabbis and scribes, they would have been literate, but not the commoners. And the first Christians were commoners."

"That makes me think of Jesus," she said, slightly shaking her head and sticking her little nose into the air, "a carpenter's son, not upper class or an intellectual, and yet the Jews back then thought it perfectly normal that he stood up in the synagogue and read from the Torah and that he would write words in the dirt that condemned those who wanted to put a poor woman to death for adultery."

"Well it's interesting to know that Jesus endorsed sexual liberties, even if it nixed the popular pastime of stoning women."

"He didn't endorse adultery. It's true that he stopped them from punishing her, but he told her to 'sin no more.'"

She now changed her stance, crossed her arms and said "Hmmph! You should know, as our illustrious Bible study leader, that one of the teaching points Jesus insisted upon is that he came into our world because forcing people to be moral through law and punishment, as in the Old Testament, had failed to make them perfect. So, killing people for adultery made no more sense than killing people for homosexuality."

Her emphasis on the last word drew attention from other tables. She seemed to thrive on creating a scene.

"Listen, Cambria," I said, "there are so many contradictions in what you're arguing. Jesus told the Roman soldiers to keep on soldiering, the Apostle Paul says the judge wears a sword to enforce capital punishment, and yet you're saying Jesus taught not to punish. I think you need—"

"There's so much confusion in your thinking process," she interrupted, "that you see contradictions where there are none. Personal sins and social sins are, once again, apples and oranges. To keep society safe and people from killing each other we need law and punishment. An adulteress is not murdering anyone, and neither is a gay person!"

More heads from more tables turned our way.

Not wanting to make a greater spectacle, I sat down, hoping Cambria would follow suit. She stood her ground, proving she was not going to make much of a submissive wife for a fundamentalist preacher. "That story about writing in the dirt," I tried to explain, "was inserted into the Gospel of John. It wasn't in it to begin with."

"Even if you're right, that doesn't mean it's a made-up story or even a late one. It still shows the Jews were more literate than others. And think about it, what did Jews do for a living back then? There were Jews in Rome and in every Greek city Paul visited. Why were they there?"

I didn't have an immediate answer, but she did.

"Because they were merchants. Merchants needed to know how to read and write to make and execute contracts and defend their interests in court."

It's odd having the roles reversed, with the student standing above and the teacher below. The only repartee I could think of was to say, "Is that all?"

That's something one should never say to a female.

"Of course not. The Puritans had a literacy rate above seventy percent according to my American history textbook. That was well before the Industrial Revolution! It's because they, like the Jews, had a holy book necessary to their lives."

"Well," I said having found a chink in Joan of Arc's armor, "the Puritans wouldn't have had such a high literacy rate without the printing press, which wasn't invented until the fifteenth century."

Cambria jutted her chin out at me, which was no great exploit for her, and asked if we were still meeting for Bible study because she had more to say.

I suddenly realized that my Bible study idea was not panning out as planned. It's not that there were no answers to Cambria's diatribes, obviously there were, it's just that I felt a bit awkward having it out with a student. The danger was that my Bible study students could become infected by her truculent attitude. Would this affect their behavior in class as well?

I mulled her question over in my head forwards and backwards, then sideways. At last I had an idea. Since we were about to broach the Roman Empire in class, whose history includes that of Jesus', I would call off the Bible study as it would be redundant to discussion in class. Of course, I knew full well that in class, given the lecture format, there was very little discussion to be had. By this time, I had become a little dreamy, relieved that I could deliver myself from a Bible study gone wrong.

"Well?" Cambria said pricking me on the back of the hand with her pen.

I felt like I had been stung, and since I suffer

from a fear of bees, technically melissophobia, which stemmed from my exploit as a ten-year old of sitting down upon a nest of bumblebees, I said whatever could come easiest and quickest out of the mouth: "Of course!"

"Good. For a moment I thought you would act cowardly about it and say something idiotic like we'll be covering the same material in class so there'll be no need for a Bible study. I think you've earned my respect." She then took up her laptop, said her au revoir to Franky, but in a very different tone than the one reserved for me, and departed.

I looked at Franky. "Are you two dating or something?"

Franky looked down at his Bible with a sheepish grin. "Nah, I wouldn't say that."

Maybe they weren't. But his flushed cheeks told me he hoped they would be.

***

After grading some papers in the adjunct office, I made my way out to the bike rack that's just beyond and left of the bottom of the steps leading down from Neal Hall. I found Tasia lingering about. It was an odd place to loiter for a bikeless person and the only conclusion I could make was that she was waiting for me.

"Watcha need?" I asked.

"Oh, I was just wondering," she said as she came up close to me and put her two hands flat on my chest and leaned toward me. "A friend of mine in the dorm said that Aspinwall has some drug dealers, and I know you're not a prig, so I was thinking, since you've been around here a couple years, you might tell me who they are."

"Well, I, ugh...don't deal with dealers," I said.

"Oh, I know you wouldn't, but it's for a paper I'm doing in sociology."

I stiffened up and tried not to move, because if I'd shifted two inches forward, I would have been kissing her. "Oh, I imagine it would be. Very interesting topic, drug dealers and drugs. Makes one lightheaded just to consider drugs, but I'm afraid I don't know of any dealers."

"You could ask around for me, couldn't you? To help me out on my paper. Perhaps some of your colleagues might know?"

"I suppose I could," I said, struggling a bit to disengage myself from her and get to my bike.

She let me go and said, rather loudly, "Thank-you so much, Tristan. You are definitely the sweetest."

I unlocked my bike chain, pulled my bike

from the rack and then launched myself upon it. As I passed the steps to Neal Hall, I saw Angela at the top of them. She smiled and acknowledged me as I waved at her, but she also looked off in the direction of Tasia, with no smile at all.

***

The next morning, upon entering Langstrom's office for coffee, I found my three fellow Miscreants seated in a triangle and all looking up at me as if I were the awaited Messiah.

"Hail to the Chief!" exclaimed our political scientist, Professor Sim Garfield.

"I could lodge some sort of complaint about an ethnic slur," I said as I sat down, "but I'm too interested in finding out what you mean by that."

Al turned to me and announced, "You can save the day."

"From what?'

"You haven't heard. Our own Dr. Sonia Abbot has been nominated for Professor of the Year. We can't let it come to pass."

"It's not the ten-thousand-dollar award that concerns us you understand," said Langstrom, "it's the principle of the thing. We can't let a wanna-be academic go parading about the halls as if this is 1921 and she's Einstein accepting the Nobel Prize."

"Well," I said, "she does get glowing reviews from the students."

"Certainly she does," said Sim, "and there is no flag more red than the one floating above a pile of student evaluations laden with such comments as 'the best professor I've ever had.'"

"Let me explain how she comes by her evaluations, Tristan," said Langstrom as he rubbed his hands together slowly, "Her grading method consists of giving a student ten points for showing up to class, another twenty for printing out a news article on the last aboriginal tribe of Brazil, thirty for watching a documentary in class..." He looked over at Al for a moment. "How many does that make?"

"Only sixty."

"Ah yes, another forty for handing in twelve words of notes summarizing the documentary. Voila, an A+. She's nothing but a poser!"

"I don't see how she keeps her job," said Al, "without ever being published."

"That's where you're wrong, my friend," Sim answered.

"And how so?" asked Al.

"Just last year," he remonstrated, "she published the program for The Social Sciences Club's annual meeting. Pulitzer stuff, that."

I was, I admit, a little adrift in their conversation, so I asked, "So how does any of this relate to me being hailed as the Chief?"

Sim reached across and gave a friendly tap to my shoulder. "Because of the cocktail party and your dear friend Tasia."

Al could tell by my sideways glance that I still hadn't a clue as to what they referred to, so he explained. "It's homecoming week and on Friday night the college president is hosting a get-together at his house. Every dean and vice-president of the college who's hoping to grasp the next rung of the administrative ladder with one hand while holding an Irish Car Bomb with the other will be there. Sonia's such a bootlicking sycophant that she'll be there twenty minutes earlier than anyone else and gone twenty minutes later than everybody else, and in between times she'll be sharing drinks with whomever she thinks might help pull or push her up the ladder. She'll be plastered by eight p.m. and won't realize it until Saturday noon when she crawls out of somebody else's bed. You'll have plenty of time to sneak into her house, get on her computer, copy her internet history, and bingo, we'll have her for something. If anyone has a skeleton in her closet, it's Sonia."

It dawned on me how much Al presently looked like Richard Nixon plotting some sort of break-in at the Watergate Hotel.

"A skeleton? That's a horrible thing to say," I said, hoping to change the subject with what aspired to be a joke. "Her mother was cremated."

Al couldn't be knocked off script. "We're counting on you."

"It's crazy," I said. "For starters, I wouldn't know how to log onto her computer."

He tapped my shoulder once more. "That's where your dear Tasia comes in. She was telling Henry here how professors should be more careful with their passwords, because she saw her sociology professor use hers on the classroom computer."

I glanced at Langstrom. "And Tasia remembered it?"

"She said it was so simple," Langstrom said. "Here, I have it written down. It was Dd051980 with two exclamation marks."

I took the sheet of paper from his hands. "She remembered Dd051980!! and she can't remember when Jesus was born?"

"She said it matched the initials and birthdate of her uncle."

Sim nodded at me enthusiastically. "Had Jesus been her uncle, I'm sure she would know when he was born."

"So," resumed Al, "take that password and be at my house around nine o'clock. That will give Sonia plenty of time to settle in at the party. You'll go to her side door and take the key from under the geranium pot. Her office is on the second floor, facing my house. Very irritating. She pulls the blinds. No doubt but that something nefarious is going on in there; and for the good of the student body, for the honor of academia, you're going to find out what!"

***

Friday seemed distant to me. I had plenty of time to contemplate my break-in at Sonia's. In the meantime, I focused on grading papers, reading about hermits, and holding class. For Wednesday, I discoursed on Alexander the Great and Aristotle, and then finished with the Stoics and Epicureans.

I highly recommended Epicureanism to the class. To be sure, it's hard to dismiss a philosophy that gives you complete freedom of action. Epicurus calls upon us to ignore the gods as much as they ignore us and to free oneself of social obligations. "Embrace pleasure and avoid pain" seems to be a motto fit for even our times. And then you think of Epicurus's supporters, like Lucretius and his tome *On the Nature of Things*. We finally have someone talking sense, someone who can explain the world without throwing in a miracle.

Of course, Cambria couldn't help herself, objecting that a self-centered life was an unfulfilled one.

"We're meant to live one for the other," she preached. "To complement each other. That's why there is marriage, a husband living for his wife and the wife for her husband."

"Well," I said, playing the devil's advocate as is fit for the skeptic, "I don't think you have to be male and female to create a marriage."

"A male marrying a male," she said with a sarcastic punch to the word marrying. "It would be like being in love with yourself. There's no effort, no true giving of self. True love is falling for someone who shares your deepest convictions but lacks what you have and has what you lack. Your fundamental problem is that you cannot accept the way that you're made, you reject your Creator!"

"No," shot back Angela, "rather it's you and your silly, bigoted ideas that he rejects!"

Angela's blast surprised me. She typically keeps a low profile in class. Now, she clearly had guns out and blazing, and we professors are not used to getting supporting fire from a student. I saw she was reloading and ready to fire off another salvo so I stepped in between her and the target.

"You're right, Angela," I said, "we shouldn't have prejudiced ideas. It's certainly against our school's mission statement. But I don't think Cambria means to be bigoted. She's just had a different upbringing than most. And that's what coming to college is for. It's to help us see the other side of things. I'm sure after a year or two, she'll have put a lot of water in her wine."

"Don't patronize me," Cambria said. "And I'm not going to be putting any water into my wine because I don't drink wine in the first place. Besides, I'm a senior now, so if your three years of brainwashing haven't cleansed me yet, I don't see how another year is going to get the job done."

The atmosphere in the classroom, by this time, had become very tense and a silence prevailed.

"Who needs brains anyway," came a voice

from behind the first row, it was Tasia's. Her comment produced laughter among her classmates and broke the tension. "Really," she said turning to the others as if to explain, "I'm happy and I get everything I need without giving it a second thought." Then she batted her eyelashes at everyone, and more laughs came forth.

I could have kissed Tasia for saving the day. To tell the truth, but without giving any credit to Cambria's theory about true love, I think I could have kissed her anyway, because it just seemed to me that we might indeed be made for each other, at least for a couple of nights.

As I looked around the class, I saw that even Cambria was amused by Tasia's antics. The only one not laughing was Angela.

7

By Thursday night, I was fully armed and ready to meet the enemy at the Bookshire Coffee and Tea Shop. I realized that I needed to regain the initiative, if ever I'd had it, by convincing these undergrads that the Jews of Jesus' day were, aside from one exception, unquestionably illiterate.

This required changing up the agenda a bit.

"Before we move on to the Gospel of Mark," I said, "I want to point out that there are several letters in the New Testament, most of which were written by the only educated man to join the early church. The man's name was Paul, sometimes known as the Apostle Paul or simply as the Apostle. He claimed to become a follower of Jesus three years after Jesus had been put to death, but he didn't become truly involved with the Christian movement until some twelve years later. During the interim, he lived in far-off

Anatolia, which took about two and a half weeks to walk to from Jerusalem. In other words, he wasn't around to take notes or anything during the first fifteen years of the movement. And he didn't write much about Jesus' earthly ministry anyway."

I could see some rustling around in the chairs occupied by my fundamentalists, but they had nothing to say, so I continued, "There are some noteworthy things that should be said about the letters Paul eventually did write."

Finally, Franky spoke up. "Paul seems to say a lot about who Jesus was."

"No," I insisted, "he says a lot about who he thought Jesus was as a spirit. Or at least that's what we think Paul wrote, but who knows. Someone could have altered his letters."

"I don't see how," Franky ventured. "It was sacred scripture."

I could see that Franky made his assertions feebly, as if he wanted to believe in what he was saying but had doubts, nonetheless. I was making progress with him.

"We must remember," I said, "that though Christians today think Paul's letters are holy writ that cannot be altered, those Christians who first received them did not consider them sacred."

I had no sooner finished saying this than Cambria let off a little steam. "I don't see how any of what you're saying proves the Jews were illiterate. On the contrary, Paul wrote his letters to be read by others. Those others had to be literate!"

I tried to be patient with her and said, more calmly than my heartrate allowed for, "Paul asked that the letters be read aloud to the congregations. You know what that implies, don't you?"

There was a silence in the other corner of the boxing ring. Obviously, they had come, gloves laced, to fight for Mark but not for Paul. Cambria had the brow narrowly furrowed and was rhythmically tapping her fingers on the table.

"It implies," I explained, "that the people in the congregations were illiterate. They had to be read to because they could not read themselves!"

This definitively shut up the opposition, so I could proceed to my next argument, which, I calculated, would open their eyes. "Since the first Christians were illiterate and didn't see the stories they heard about Jesus as sacred and immutable, what do you think would happen?"

Quinton spoke up. "Those guys would start

adding to the stories and pretty soon you would have contradictions."

"Yes," I said. "The stories would be similar but with variations, sometimes to the point that they give conflicting information. You can see this when you read the gospels. You may have noticed that Matthew, Mark, and Luke have similar but contrasting stories about Jesus. If you read the texts closely, it's obvious Mark was the first one to write down the Jesus tales and then Matthew and Luke copied him while adding in more information to the stories that had been invented since Mark first penned his gospel." I did add, to assuage the feelings of my fundamentalists, that creative plagiarism was not a crime in the Roman Empire and was practiced by both academics and religionists.

We then began the Bible study in earnest, going through the opening chapters of Mark. I pointed out that even by that late date, the author had not yet thought of a nativity story for Jesus, but he did include the tale of angels attending to Jesus in the desert, before Jesus set off to collect his disciples and miraculously heal people.

"It is noteworthy that his miracles could be practical," I said, for laughs. "Nothing worse than coming into a house where the woman there is too sick to cook. Such was the case, you see in verses thirty and thirty-one, of Peter's mother-in-law, who was in bed with a fever. Seeing this, Jesus had her up and out of bed and cooking in no time."

"What an exploiter," said Tasia with genuine spite.

Cambria looked at Tasia. At first, I thought I saw anger in Cambria's eyes, but upon closer inspection it looked more like a cross between worry and pity. "Perhaps," said Cambria, "Peter's mother-in-law desperately wanted to welcome Jesus but couldn't, and Jesus helped her up so she would be free to do what she wanted to do. To love, honor, and serve a fellow human being. Don't you have that desire, Tasia?"

Tasia was caught off guard by the personal question. It seemed to be too personal. "It's a dog eat dog world out there, honey," she said. "You'd better learn to fend for yourself or you'll be in the doggy dish. Nobody is out there doing something good for another without wanting something more in return. Believe me. Been there, tried that."

"You see, Tasia," said Cambria, "you started out in life knowing that was the right thing to do, to live for others—"

"Don't preach at me!" Tasia interjected, perhaps a little louder than she meant. "I'm sorry, Cambria, you and I just walk down different paths. How about you Professor Telsmith? Do you live for others or yourself?"

"Well, I would hope I live for others as well as myself. I don't think the two are incompatible."

"Of course not," said Cambria, who for the first time seemed to look approvingly at me. "It's understood that Jesus expects you to take care of yourself, to get your daily bread and all that, you can see it in his parables. The farmer who properly sows his wheat, the farmer who wisely oversees his harvest, etc. We're expected to conscientiously carry out our vocations here on earth, but it doesn't mean we don't help and share with those around us. If we don't, we're all alone, miserable in the end. We were created to love and serve others."

Tasia didn't answer. She blinked and looked down at her phone, now disinterested in the conversation.

"So," I said to bring the Bible study to a close, "in this spirit of neighborly and kindly thoughts, I think it's time we end our inquiries into the Holy Book for the night. Thank you all for coming and I'll see you in class tomorrow."

Campus Menace — Preston Shires

***

On Friday, I returned to the classroom with a good seventy percent of my respect restored, which is a passing grade. Unfortunately, in lecture, we had reached the first century AD, and I was obliged to mention the arrival of Christianity and I couldn't help repeating what I'd said at Bible Study: how the Jesus stories were imperfectly passed along from one person to the next by word of mouth until they were finally written down by second class scribes.

"You, being college students, can clearly understand the implication of this. Because people wanted to believe in a wonder worker, the originally mundane things that Jesus did, became, over the decades, transformed into miracle stories."

"Imagine," I said, "a multitude of people, perhaps a hundred, following Jesus up into the hills. Dinner time arrives and Peter's mother-in-law is not there to cook. Jesus' devotees, the disciples, note that though they have five loaves of bread and two fish, they'll never be able to stuff the stomachs of so many hangers-on, so the disciples tell their teacher to send the people home. Jesus, knowing that people don't traipse about the countryside having nothing upon them more than a toga, ignores their request, pronounces a dinner prayer, and then instructs his disciples to start eating their five loaves and two fish. The other people, following the example, dig into their baskets, pull out what bread and fish they have, and those who have more than enough share with their neighbors and everyone is satisfied.

"In time, this story, being passed on from one person to the next, and always with a measure of embellishment, transforms itself into a miracle, wherein Jesus and the disciples were the only ones who had bread and fish, but Jesus miraculously made the five loaves and two fish multiply in great enough quantity to fill the paunches of four to five thousand people."

I was about to continue on when I couldn't help but see a hand waving in my face from the front row.

"Yes, Cambria?" I asked with a measure of trepidation.

"Did your mother ever receive a letter from your grandmother?"

"I don't remember, I believe my grandmother sent emails," I answered judiciously.

"How about the history club? Aren't you the

faculty advisor?"

"You mean The Social Sciences Club? Yes, I am. It's a distinguished title conferred, for some reason, upon the lowest level adjunct professor."

"Yeah, you gave out scholarships for history majors."

"Oh," I said relieved, "you want to apply?"

"No, I just know that Angela won one of your scholarships and that she wrote the club a thank-you note."

"That's true," I said nodding at Angela, "a well written note, which I did read out to the members of the honor society at the August meeting."

"Gotcha!"

Like the students in the class, I looked at her inquisitively.

"Gotcha?" I asked.

"Yes, it would have been time consuming, inefficient, and just plain silly to hand the note around and wait for each person to read it for himself."

"Yes," I said, acknowledging her logic, but wondering if a centimorgan of insanity hadn't filtered down into her genome.

"I'm not quite sure what this has to do with my grandmother," I said.

"It has nothing to do with her and everything to do with mine, who is old-fashioned and still writes us letters that come in the form of ink on paper. Whenever we receive one, my mother takes us into the living room and reads it out to us because it's addressed to the whole family. That got me thinking, that's all."

"It's good to think," I said encouragingly.

"And the same thing applied in the first century. My goodness, it would have taken three months to get every Christian in Rome to work through Paul's epistle to them. Just because someone read Paul's letter out loud to the congregation of the church it was addressed to doesn't prove Jewish illiteracy any more than I could prove the members of The Social Sciences Club are illiterate."

The penny dropped and I realized she was not insane but had rather sprung another one of her ambushes.

"It still does not negate the illiteracy of the Jews," I pointed out coolly. "For argument's sake, just consider that Jewish commoners, like all their neighbors, were unable to read and write. How would you share that letter with them? There's only one way, which is?"

"To read it out loud to them," said Tasia.

I had to confess inwardly that Tasia's

intelligence seemed to be catching up with her undeniable attractiveness.

"In any case," I concluded, "the basic fact is that no gospel was written before 69 AD, some forty years after Jesus was put to death, which means most of those who had seen Jesus were themselves dead by the time the gospels were written. And, to top it off, the Jesus stories we have in the gospels were created up in Anatolia, modern-day Turkey, far from Palestine where Jesus had carried out his ministry."

Having cleared up the matter to my satisfaction, I dumped a little bad news on the class to dampen their spirits.

"Remember you should be reading ahead for your book report, which is to be on a primary source. I'll put some of these at the reference desk in the library for you to check out. Class dismissed."

***

I had not forgotten my Friday night duty, and I must admit that with the week coming to an end and school spirit at its height for the homecoming, I felt energized and looked forward to a bit of breaking and entering. Besides, life can get dull on a nightly diet of hermits and westerns.

Indeed, I chucked aside the persona of John Wayne altogether, not seeing him as a smooth cloak-and-dagger-lock-picking kind of man, but rather the cowboy-boot-to-the-door kind of man who only breaks in if there's a house full of ruffians to knock silly. Instead, I chose the James Bond type, rather suave, like Moore, whatever his first name is. I'm sure it's not Dudley. No name starting with 'dud' could be cast for the part.

Anyway, I reported to Al's house, awaited the opportune moment and then stealthily divested the geranium pot of its key. I was inside in a sneeze, wandering about like a cat burglar who forgot his flashlight. I found the waste basket three times and picked up its contents twice. I saw no point in doing it more than necessary.

The floating counter Sonia keeps between refrigerator and sink, rolling about on its wheels, was obviously there to stop the faint-hearted intruder, but I am not of that ilk. I butted into it more than one could knock over a waste basket and yet I finally negotiated my way around it and found the stairs.

Having learned my lesson about walking upright, when I first discovered the corner of the floating counter with my groin, I climbed slowly up the stairs on all fours, rubbing up against the wall as I proceeded as any experienced blind man would do.

Now, why Sonia would have placed a rather tall plant stand at the head of the stairs, and on the left side, I have no idea, unless she feared a blind burglar. That must have been her thinking, because when my forehead found it, the stand itself vacated the spot and the plant atop it came my way. I didn't mind the plant tumbling down on my head as much as the pot containing it.

I shook off the plant and its *terra infirma* and made my way up to a hallway with hardwood flooring. My every step was accompanied by a sharp squeak from my tennis shoes. Now I understood why Bond always wore dress shoes.

Knowing that Sonia would be safely imbibing drink for some time before taking the wheel home, and that the upstairs hallway was hidden from view, I flicked on my phone light in order to find the door to her study.

Once inside her den, I extricated the paper with the secret code from my pocket, laid it on the table, and illuminated it with my phone, which was in my left hand, and typed away, one click at a time, with the forefinger of my right hand.

I was about to hit 'ENTER' when I heard another click. It was far off, downstairs. I thumbed off the phone light and tiptoed to the doorway. Squeak, squeak, squeak.

"I'm sure we saw a light on in your house." It wasn't Sonia's voice, but it was one known to me.

"Well I'm glad you let me know, Tasia," came another voice, definitely belonging to Sonia, "I'll take a look."

"Do you want us to stay here?" came a man's voice.

"Yes, Barton," said Sonia, "if you would, while I have a look around upstairs."

I took off my sneakers and retreated to the far end of the hallway and slipped into an open doorway. I could hear her climbing the stairs. She paused at the landing, probably thinking a blind man had been crawling about her house. I heard her enter her office, where she must have paced around her desk a time or two, and then exit by closing the door. The sound of the heels of her shoes hitting the hardwood echoed toward me, getting louder and louder. I dropped my tennis shoes and felt around in the dark for something to hide in or behind. All I could find was a bed, so I climbed in and pulled the covers up over myself.

The sound of footsteps halted. I sensed more than heard a finger switch on the light. I was brave, I don't believe I trembled. I lay as still and quiet as the mattress, hoping to blend in.

"Well, well," I heard a soft voice say gently. "If someone hasn't removed his shoes to await me. I wonder what else he's taken off."

The rudeness with which Sonia pulled the covers from my face took me by surprise.

"Hi," I said weakly, "I was tired."

Sonia stepped out into the hallway, calling down to Tasia and Barton, "It's all right, I forgot that my brother was coming to spend the night. You can let yourselves out. Thank you."

She returned to the bedroom and waited for the front door to shut. "I do have a brother, you know," she said while nodding at a picture frame filled with the image of herself and a wardrobe of a man standing next to her, big, mean looking, and not smiling.

"Oh, I don't see why not. Many sisters have brothers."

"Only mine lives just fifteen minutes from here."

"Is he a big brother?" I asked, sitting up in bed and taking a serious interest in her family tree.

"No, but he does wear a badge."

"Spelling bee winner, is he?"

"No, marksman, but the badge is for sheriff."

"That's too bad, people often find it hard to spell sheriff. Is it 'f-f' or 'r-r'? You see if he had been the spelling bee—"

"I regret to say," she said brusquely, no doubt anxious to get back to the party and finish off her margarita, "but I am calling him now." She pulled out her phone and swiped it.

"Oh, I can spell it for him if that's the problem."

"I'll tell you what," she added as her finger hovered over the phone. "I'll not make the call if you tell me what you were doing here and who put you up to whatever you're up to. I could see that you had been in my study messing with my computer."

"It's not a conspiracy. I just wanted to see your lesson plans. You see I was considering having my students get so many points for doing certain things, perhaps ten points for showing up to class, another twenty for printing out a news article on the last aboriginal tribe of Brazil, thirty for watching a documentary, forty for—"

"Henry put you up to this. Henry

Langstrom." There wasn't a hint of supposition in her voice.

"Well," I confessed as much as I needed to without the sheriff being present, "he did say you have a unique grading system."

"He wanted you to find dirt on me through my computer to destroy my chances for getting the Professor of the Year Award."

"We think awards should be shared."

"Listen, Tristan, I'm going to let you go." She said this as she pointed her phone in my general direction and took a picture of me in her bed. "However, I'm still going to call my little but big brother. He's going to take fingerprints and the whole nine-yards."

"That won't get him a first down, you know."

"Not unless I tell him to make the arrest. I'll have the goods on you, as they say in your gangster movies."

"Westerns, but they often still get the goods on someone, so I follow."

"And then your little teaching career will come to an end and you'll begin a new one down at Stickers. You and Chris will make an admirable pair of waiters."

"Should I get you a hamburger and fries now, or?"

"I'm not going to prosecute you, my dear

Tristan, if you behave yourself and perform a small something for me." She paused and extracted from the pocket of her blazer jacket the paper that had her password written on it, something I probably should not have left on her desk.

She resumed, saying, "The little favor I alluded to earlier in the hallway of the Neal building." She then proceeded to go into some detail about what she expected of me.

Once she was done, I tried to explain to her that being a double agent would not be an easy task, even James Bond knew where to draw the line in this respect; but Sonia had infinite confidence in my capabilities.

My mission, which I had no choice but to accept, was to infiltrate Langstrom's office, which wouldn't be difficult over the noon hour, provided the door was open, which it wouldn't be, and then run through his computer and emails for anything connected to the codeword "Robert Jones."

It's the latter part of the mission, of course, that would prove the challenge, but what bothered me equally was that "Robert Jones" didn't sound like much of a codeword. Something catchier, like "Operation Torch," would have motivated me more.

So, I was not in the chirpiest of moods as Sonia escorted me downstairs to the side door. On my way out, as she kept an eye on me, I gently lifted the geranium pot and deposited the key. I rose and bid her good night. She blew me a kiss.

Coming out onto the sidewalk I distinctly thought I heard movement in the hedge separating Al's and Sonia's houses. I looked down both sides but the darkness, being true to itself, revealed nothing. I had no ambition to explore the phenomenon lest there be another cat burglar on the prowl who had forgotten his flashlight by confusing it with a bludgeon.

The thought quickly left my brain and settled in my feet, which picked up their pace. I wouldn't say I broke into a jog, but I did walk faster than any jog I've ever performed.

Back home at the kitchen table, I sat much like I had on a previous night, with three fingers of redeye in hand. I really should stop watching westerns.

Stanley sauntered in and noted that my crest had fallen by quite a bit.

"Home early? I would have thought you would have been at the to-do at the college president's house."

"Never got that far. Didn't have an invitation."

"How far did you get?"

"As far as Sonia Abbot's bed."

"Isn't she a bit old for you?"

"Yes, Mother," I said dryly.

Stanley took up a chair across from me. "I think you'd better tell me about it before you empty my bottle of whiskey."

Stanley and I don't run around in the same circle of friends, so I told him of my dilemma.

"You need to put the con on 'em my man," said Stanley, taking on his imperfect gangsta accent. "You weave your web and draw 'em in, bite them passwords. You can do it. That's the way we does it back in the hood."

"Stanley, you may be black, but you're from Lincoln, Nebraska. Your mother's a CPA and your dad's a real estate broker."

"I know, but I used to live with my aunt and uncle in Detroit."

"No, you didn't, you went up there once every two years for Thanksgiving."

"Well, I was alive, so I was living there."

"Anyway, in Nebraskanese, what are you saying?"

"Oh," he said recalibrating. "We was

thinking—"

"Your Nebraskanese."

"Ok...I was thinking, if you could get your buddies up there at the college to discuss passwords in general, they might just say how the best way is to make up a password."

"That sounds like a wonderful plan if I'm applying for an IT job."

"No, just think a second, if they tell you what the best way is, then they'll be revealing how they came up with their passwords. Once you've figured out what Langstrom's password might be, you jam some chewing gum into the door latch, and when everyone's gone, you come back and 'Voila!' the door opens. You get inside, get what you need out of his computer, take out the gum, and deliver the goods to Dr. Abbot."

I thought over his plan for a moment and I couldn't come up with a better one myself. Finally, I grabbed a glass, generously poured him a shot of his whiskey and handed it to him. "Here's to the hood," I said as we clinked glasses.

***

The following Monday morning I strolled into the Miscreant HQ and took up my position.

After the usual pleasantries, Al grilled me.

"So how did things work out at Sonia's; any good dirt?"

I shook my head negatively, "I think she changes her password every week."

"But you still could have found something," Langstrom remonstrated. "Always in the movies they guess the password. They think of the person's birth date or something, tap away, hit enter, and they're in. You don't have to be James Bond to do that."

"I watch westerns."

"True," said Al. "No help there."

"Do you guys use your birth dates?" I asked innocently.

Sim Garfield confessed with a sad nod.

"I've moved beyond that," Langstrom bragged. "Marriage date."

"I thought you were getting a divorce? After all, you're here and she's up in Nebraska City," Al said, surprised.

"It reminds me it's all coming to an end soon. I don't know how I ever got entangled with her. She had to be the most boring person to have ever been granted a college degree, even those who got a degree in accounting. When the divorce is finalized, I'll adjust my password."

Professor Garfield, continuing with his

somber mood, complained, "I wish the IT people wouldn't make everybody change his blasted password once a year and mix odd characters into the recipe. I've got the numbers of my birthdate all inverted and I've had to add a couple of exclamation marks!"

"I love putting in the exclamation marks," Langstrom countered.

I was rather proud of my strategy for outing everyone's password-creating technique, but their switching around of numbers and throwing in the odd exclamation point took some of the wind out of my pride.

Nevertheless, the game was afoot. All I needed was a date of marriage and a list of all the numerical combinations thereof. Having established a game plan, I rose and asked off-handedly, "Does anyone have any gum?"

***

By Thursday night I had purchased a packet of gum at the convenience store next to the Bookshire.

I opened the Bible study session by reemphasizing that when the New Testament documents were first written, they didn't have the status they do today, and scribes felt at liberty to alter the wording to better fit the teachings of Jesus as they understood them.

Cambria, unsurprisingly, jumped in immediately. "Why wouldn't they consider Paul's letters as sacred and unalterable?"

Tasia rolled her eyes, but I was ready for fundamentalism. "You must understand that Christians think of the Scriptures that way today because the New Testament has been canonized and respected for some 1,700 years. Back then, though, the gospels and epistles were fresh and new."

"The latest New York Times best seller is fresh and new, but I wouldn't change its wording and resell it as the original."

I looked her in the eyes. They were bright and energetic, and one might even suspect charming. But taken as an ensemble with her prominent jaw and sharpish tongue, the word charming was quickly replaced with tedious and nitpicky.

"Of course not," I explained, feeling as if I were unlocking a door that was already gapingly open, "because we have copyright laws today, which means newly published works can't be manipulated. Even a scholar can't copy word for word somebody else's writing or he'll be defrocked for plagiarizing. Like I said before, plagiarism wasn't looked down upon back then. And we historians are somewhat thankful for that because that's how we know much of Livy's *History of Rome*. His successors plagiarized him, albeit they added things here and there, where they wanted to. Christian copyists did the same thing with the gospels and letters before they were collected, canonized, and shoved into something we now call the New Testament."

"There you go again," said Cambria, "confusing pagans and Jews. For the Jews, the written word of God was sacred. To change it was an offense against God, an invitation for divine punishment." She then put that jaw of hers up into the air for emphasis and declared, with a hint of what one can only identify as nasality in tone, "I think the Dead Sea scrolls should have taught you that."

I looked at Tasia and for anybody else who might want to slap her but there were no takers. "The Dead Sea scrolls, Cambria, were copies of old biblical books, books that had been sanctified by time. Paul's letters were, I say again, fresh and new."

Cambria held her breath, but her mind was spinning something up, I could see it in those deceptive eyes. "So," she finally asked, "are you saying nothing said today can be considered sacred, unalterable?"

I tilted my head, pushed out my lower lip, and lifted my eyebrows to indicate that I doubted very much that someone today could come up with a gospel out of the blue.

"Have you ever been to a Pentecostal meeting?"

I couldn't say that I had been, or ever would be.

"The Pentecostals," she said looking around the table at everyone, "believe that the Holy Spirit speaks through them today."

Tasia looked at Cambria with a smirk. "And why not? I make my own rules."

"I'm sure you do," said Cambria caustically. "But they don't because Scripture says no one can add or take away from the Bible. If it didn't say that they would probably, like you probably do, staple their beliefs right onto the last page of Revelations. So," she turned to me and asked, "how can you say that first century Jewish Christians couldn't think that Paul's writing had the blessing of God, especially when the Apostle said most everything he wrote was from the Lord?"

"If we're going to trust these documents like you seem to, then we have to note that the Apostle didn't always say he spoke from the

Lord."

"True, but he specified when he was just giving his opinion."

"But," I asked as I thumbed through the Bible to the Gospel of Mark, "is it always easy to tell where his opinion starts and where it leaves off? It's too bad this hadn't been resolved by the scribes before they canonized the New Testament."

I kept talking and had to cut Cambria off twice lest the Bible study continue on until everyone fell asleep during the wee hours of the morn. Having finally regained control, I took up my copy of the New Testament and showed the students how many of Mark's passages also appeared in Matthew and Luke, reemphasizing how the latter two evangelists had plagiarized the former.

I concluded my lesson by pointing out, once again, that since Mark was the first gospel, and therefore written around 69 AD, then Matthew and Luke were probably composed in the 80s AD, given the fact that the Marcan stories they repeated had evolved somewhat before the "publication" of their gospels. In any case, all the gospels were written long after Jesus had died.

With my educational mission accomplished,

I dismissed my biblical scholars and waited in line at the counter for a take-away hot chocolate. When I exited the coffee shop, I saw Franky in the distance. Leaning on his arm was Tasia. He didn't seem to be objecting and I concluded there was no stopping Eros once his arrow had left the bow. I wasn't about to go home and fetch the cheese. I'd learned my lesson.

Observing this budding and curious romance between a fundamentalist nerd and a shameless tease, I noted out of the corner of my eye an advancing female figure, moving stealthily forward, keeping close to the hedge lining the sidewalk. If the two turned around she could easily press herself into the greenery and remain unseen. It was Cambria, like a cat, stalking the lovebirds.

9

I figured Monday morning would be the day of reckoning. I knew all the Miscreants' schedules, and all I had to do was plug the door latch hole in the doorjamb and return when I knew they'd all be gone, which would be between twelve-thirty and one-thirty. They had a habit of meeting up in Langstrom's office and leaving their phones there before marching over to the cafeteria. There was no greater sin for a Miscreant than to look at one's phone during the lunchtime social hour.

I made sure to chew my four sticks of gum before entering Langstrom's office to chat around the coffee pot. As any good spy would tell you, I didn't want anyone suspecting me of chewing gum, so I made use of my tongue and shoved it into the vacancy between cheek and wisdom tooth, something evolution had created in us for just such a moment as this.

Sim Garfield eyed me carefully, like a colleague one doesn't know very well looks at you in a board meeting and doesn't quite know how to tell you that you've got a dab of mayonnaise hanging off your right cheek.

The distraction for Sim proved too much for him and he finally had to address the issue. "Have you got an infected jaw?"

I lifted my hand and felt a noticeable bump. I winced. "Yes, I'm to see the dentist this week."

"Good God," he said, "you should go today. Otherwise you'll be needing an infection on the other side to reestablish your facial symmetry."

"Let me see," said Al. He pressed on the protrusion. I winced again. "It's spongy. You don't want the infection to spread. Sim's right, you go today. Who's your dentist?"

"Novak, I believe, unless I'm confusing his name with that anesthetic."

Langstrom had gone to the search engine. "No, you're not. Here it is: Dr. Novak, DDS, Auburn, Nebraska."

In no time, thanks to Sim's quick fingers on his phone, I had an appointment for early afternoon.

You might think this would have put me in a fix, but I had read my Candide, and in that story Professor Pangloss teaches us that all things ultimately work out for the better. I took heed and said to my friends, while holding my jaw, "I doubt I'll be able to make it to lunch."

I rose from my chair and leaned toward the door while looking at the far shelf. The titles of the books were beyond the reach of my Clark Kent glasses. Nevertheless, I said, "Oh, I wanted to borrow that book of yours on the top shelf. One of the students was asking about it." All three professors scanned the shelf. Meanwhile, I coughed the gum into my hand and jammed it into the doorjamb. It was not an easy task as the hole seemed to be smaller than my wad of gum.

Langstrom finally got up to take a closer look at his shelves. "Which one you say? This one?" he asked posing his hand upon a title.

I could have said "Yes" but that would not have had the ring of authenticity that a good lie must generate, so I said, "No, the one three over, to the right."

"Biblical Sex?"

"That's it," I said, unsurely, as I reached out to receive the little volume.

"It's basically a picture book, mind you."

"Well," I said, thinking on my feet, "with the reading level of incoming freshmen these days, I thought it would be easier to understand."

***

At twelve-thirty sharp I slipped into Langstrom's office and closed the door behind me. I needed to work quickly because they would be back within the hour, plus I had a dentist appointment at two. I looked down at my list of password combinations, sat down, and then typed away like Rimsky-Korsakov trying to finish "Flight of the Bumblebee" before some melissophobic slammed the fallboard down on his fingers.

The first password didn't work. Neither did the second. I tried the third. I went to the fourth and was locked out.

"Hmmm..." I looked over his desk, it was as messy as my bedroom floor, but I did find his cell phone.

Surprisingly, it had no password. I thumbed through his "recently called" list: "Sim Garfield, obviously Simeon Garfield, and a host of other names, always the first and last name. Nothing indicated a Robert Jones. There was, however, an MM. I thought this odd, just two initials, so I copied the number down on an index card and stuck it in my wallet.

That's the best I could do, so I cracked open the door, jutted my head out and looked left and right. The coast being clear, I dug out my piece of gum from the doorjamb and, in the process, discovered why it had been so hard to pack the gum into the hole earlier: There already was a wad of gum in there. Green rather than white but gum nonetheless.

***

I must reiterate that Pangloss has a point. If it hadn't been for erroneously being accused of having an abscessed tooth, I would never have had a dentist's appointment, and if I had never had a dentist's appointment, I would have been obliged to eat lunch with the Miscreants and would not have been able to rifle through Langstrom's affairs. More importantly, I would not have discovered I had two serious cavities that Dr. Novak insisted on drilling out root and branch, as they say, and backfilling with dental cement. It would have been convenient had the cavities placed themselves on the correct jawbone, in line with where I'd had the protrusion of gum, but one must accept some exceptions in Pangloss' theorem in order to prove his rule.

If Monday morning's class had proved pleasant, it was due to the midterm I administered. The pleasantness, I admit, was one of perspective, but the good vibes reverberating in my heart stimulated my search of Langstrom's office and endured through the encounter with the dentist, and on through the rest of the afternoon. The gladness and general sense of wellbeing even inspired me to take my evening meal at Stickers, with the understanding that all of the chewing would have to be executed on one side of the mandible.

Chris turned up to be my waiter. I had no grudge against him, he was a good fellow, even a decent adjunct as far as I knew. He certainly did not deserve what had happened to him.

"You ever think about hopping back into academia?" I asked. "Writing a thunderous monograph that sends you soaring over the heads of those who have besmirched your name?"

Chris set his cleaning rag on the table and slid into a chair beside me to share something in confidence.

"I do have plans, my friend. I understand there is to be the annual Social Sciences Club meeting here, in the not too distant future, followed by a get-together at Dr. Abbot's place. You'll be at the meeting, won't you?"

"Yes, as faculty adviser. And I plan to give a

mini-lecture about hermits."

"Good, because while the meeting is going on here, I would like to drop off a surprise at Dr. Abbot's house. I would need a car to get there and back before anyone notices I'm gone."

"I take it the 'surprise' is a gift of sorts."

"Oh, yes."

"Does it involve French cheese?"

"No," he said getting up and standing back a pace, offended. "It's a practical present for her house, and something she can use."

"Why would you be giving her a present?"

"Well, I heard her birthday is coming up, so I wanted to give her something impressive. It's been pretty tough on me since I lost my position at the college. I wasn't cut out for waiting tables."

"So, it's an olive branch you're extending to her. Knowing Sonia, she'll just cut it off and burn it."

"Probably," he said pitifully.

It must be said that I'd never heard a word pronounced more forlornly than his "probably," even when said by someone shedding a tear.

"But," Chris added as he rallied his spirits, "it will make me feel better, knowing that I at least tried to make an impression on her."

I couldn't refuse him; the car was his. He

thanked me and trundled off to wipe down a table.

His fall from grace made me think of Abelard, the medieval professor disgraced by his father-in-law and by Saint Bernard of Clairvaux. I wasn't thinking so much of what his father-in-law did to him. Chris was, I imagine, fully intact as a man, but certainly Sonia might be playing the role of Saint Bernard, who shunted the scholar off to an isolated monastery so that he might not plant his seed of thought in young scholarly minds.

***

I didn't stay long for coffee in Langstrom's office on Tuesday morning. Al was missing. He had headed off to meet with a Boston publisher who was promoting his latest play. I think I didn't stay long because his departure cast a pall of some sort. It was kind of like the three mousquetaires banding together, with myself being d'Artagnon, to defend their honor and finding Porthos absent.

Besides, I had to place some primary sources on reserve in the library.

The library, which is across the quad from Neal Hall, was once a chapel, built back in the day before educators had heard of the First Amendment. Later, in the 1920s, when it was realized that religion did not encourage teenagers to enroll in college, more pragmatic leaders transformed it into a gym with a basketball court, and in the basement, a swimming hole.

Hosting competitive sports in a chapel seemed sacrilegious to some, and so, as I've said elsewhere, someone hired a group of local farmers, experienced in putting up machine sheds, to build our present gym.

Once the athletes had been removed, someone realized that the old building's solemn ambiance fit the temperament of those rare but essential students who while away their hours quietly reading books and meditating ideas drawn therefrom. So, the swimming pool was filled in, and in no time the basement and sanctuary were christened anew as Beacon Library, in honor of an old abolitionist magazine once published in the region.

As I entered the renovated building, I noted Angela was working at a table with a pile of books at her elbow. It was no surprise. What was a surprise was to see Stanley saunter in, looking about wide-eyed as if this had been his first experience in a library.

Glancing around, his eyes finally came to rest on the object of his desire, Angela. He was totally oblivious to anyone else in the library and began a rather serpentine path toward the girl's table, stopping along the way to take a book off the shelf, flip through the pages, and then set it back.

I couldn't bear to miss the scene, so I ducked between two rows of shelves, walked to the far end and then doubled back to where I would be just a row beyond Angela's table.

I arrived before Stanley had put book number twelve back on the shelf.

"Oh, hi! Angela," he said, as if surprised to see her there.

"Hi, Stanley," she responded, without looking up from the book in front of her and her pen dancing across a sheet of paper as she took notes.

"Umm, are you studying for Tristan's class?"

She stopped writing and turned to him. "Yes, well, sort of. I'm looking into this whole Bible thing. I don't know where Cambria gets all her ideas, but I thought Tristan, um...Professor Telsmith, needed someone else in the class, besides just himself, to show how off track she is in this day and age."

"Oh, yes. Tristan's really into that stuff," said

Stanley as he permitted himself to sit down across from her.

"Well it's important."

"Yeah, lots of things are important. Like going to plays, movies, and concerts."

"What kind of movies does he like?"

"Oh, Tristan?" Stanley didn't have to think much about this since he saw me daily watching, or rather studying, films. "Old films. Not the films we watch."

"Well, I can understand. The old films seemed smarter, perhaps because of the censorship laws. They just hinted at things or used innuendoes and challenged the audience to figure out what they meant. Now, we just throw it all out there with four-letter words and naked bodies and formula plots."

"Right, then you should come over some time and we can watch one of those oldies."

"Really? Tristan would want that?"

Stanley looked at her inquisitively for a moment before saying hesitantly, like he was trying to find the words that she might expect, "Yes...he likes to watch movies...with others."

"He's shy isn't he. It's true, he's a professor and all, so you would expect him to be self-confident, but he's not like the others, is he?"

"Yeah, he's a bit shy I suppose."

"Well," she said, "I'd better get back to work, but you just tell him to pick a day and time and I'll be over."

Stanley took the hint and rose from his chair, confirming, "So you'll come? That's great. I'll let Tristan know."

While he strode away looking rather gleeful, I retraced my steps and furtively left the library.

***

On Wednesday, in the classroom, the tables had turned, metaphorically speaking. I attempted to introduce the *Pax Romana*, but any mention of peace, Roman or otherwise, was suppressed by Cambria's salvos.

"Why 69 AD?" she asked. "That's so arbitrary."

I knew she alluded to the date of composition for the Gospel of Mark, but I tried to elude her by elaborating on 69 AD as the "Year of the Four Emperors."

For her part, she knew I deviated with intent, so she only let me get as far as Emperor Galba, the first of the four, before she interrupted me by saying, "I'm not asking about the four emperors, I'm asking about the four evangelists: Matthew, Mark, Luke, and John.

Why 69 AD? And why would Mark be the first to write a gospel?"

"The general consensus," I explained, "even by Bible-believing theologians, is that Mark's gospel comes first."

"Nonsense. Not according to Mr. Rotlib, my high school Bible teacher."

This amused me, that she would bring up a high school teacher with, no doubt, a BA from Bible Believers' University, or some such, as her source. I couldn't imagine what fables Mr. Rotlib placed his faith in, and with curiosity trumping my common sense, I asked, "And what does Mr. Rotlib say?"

"He says you don't start with the unknown to get to the known. You start with the known and it can make the unknown, known."

"I don't follow."

"It's easy to tell when Luke wrote his gospel. So, we start with that."

"Yes, he probably wrote it in 85 AD."

"No, you're only saying that because you think he used Mark to write his gospel and you think Mark was written in 69 AD, no earlier. But if you put that unsubstantiated belief aside, you can figure out when Luke wrote his gospel."

"Can you now? And dismiss, in one fell swoop, two hundred years of modern biblical scholarship?"

"Certainly, by honestly answering this question: What is it that Luke left out of his second book, The Book of Acts?"

"His name, for one," I suggested.

"That's so lame. Do you find Abraham Lincoln's name in the Gettysburg Address? Franky," she called out twisting around in her seat.

Franky, not wishing to be in the spotlight, stared at her with eyes agape, if that's the word I want. I mean, to say "wide open" would not convey the deep emptiness they exhibited.

Cambria waited for the answer, but while she waited, something else caught her attention. She wasn't looking exactly at Franky but at the floor beside his feet. I immediately recognized Tasia's lavender backpack.

I looked around the room for Tasia and realized she was missing.

"Ummm," Franky stammered. "Paul's execution?"

There was a pause before Cambria, gathering her thoughts, whipped back around and exclaimed "Exactly! And why? Because it hadn't happened yet. There's no other reason why Luke would not include it. It would have been the perfect ending for his book, the climax: Paul takes the gospel to Rome, the center of the world, delivers it, and then faithful to his Master, Jesus Christ, dies a martyr for the Truth."

"Maybe he left it out," I said half listening to myself and half wondering where Tasia was, "because it would have shamed the movement to have the imperial government judge Paul a criminal and execute him."

"I don't believe it."

"You believe Luke would have included Paul's execution?"

"Yes."

"Well," I said to end the little debate, "putting unsubstantiated beliefs aside, we will proceed to cover the *Pax Romana*, but before we do. Has anyone seen Tasia?"

"Plenty of times," Angela said under her breath.

"Franky?" I asked. "Isn't that her backpack by you?"

"Uh, yes."

"So, where is the owner?"

"She said she had to go see her grandmother and had me take her to the airport early this morning. She left her backpack in my pickup, so I was going to give it to her roommate."

"Oh," said Cambria, "I can take it to

Jennifer."

"An absentee student?" I asked rhetorically, to transition back into the lecture. "An absentee," I repeated. "This brings us back to Nero, the absentee emperor who preferred to go on tour in Greece as a rock star rather than tend to the business of Empire. Great success as a musician, considering that his audiences always stayed to the end of his performances, which one hopes was due to his melodious voice, rather than to the fact that he had guards blocking the exits. In any case, by disregarding his imperial duties, and let this be a lesson to us as scholars, he lost the confidence of the senators, his peers, and was ousted."

By reintroducing Nero, I was able to run through the "Year of the Four Emperors," the successors of Nero, and then on to the remaining Flavians and the close of the first century before Cambria could reroute the lecture.

When class was over, I loitered about to see if Cambria would give a lecture of her own to Franky.

"So," Cambria said as she picked up the backpack, "did she pay you for the drive up?"

"I was just doing it to be nice."

"All the way to Eppley Airport?"

"Well, not at first. I mean, I misunderstood. It was early and I wasn't awake. She said her cousin just called to let her know her grandmother was in serious condition. I thought her grandmother was in Nebraska City, but she was just meeting some lady in Nebraska City on the way up."

"Where?"

"At a coffee shop at the edge of town."

"Why?"

"Maybe a job interview. I don't know."

"Who was it?"

"No idea. Didn't even see her. I stayed in the pickup, guarding her backpack and her little suitcase that were in the bed."

"Why did she have her backpack along?"

"'Cause she had things in it she needed for the trip. I mean when we got to the airport, she transferred some things out of it and into her carry-on."

"And Tasia didn't tell you anything about the lady at the coffee shop?"

"Not really, except that she said the lady told her to meet her there at six a.m. sharp, because that's where she had coffee and a scone every morning.

"And when she got back into the pickup, she said the woman didn't age well. Still putting on bright lipstick, when she was at the age when you don't want people realizing you don't have lips anymore."

"How charming. Tasia does have a way with words. Did she get the job?"

"I don't know, I was just guessing that's what was going on. It's only after she got back in the pickup that I figured out from her that she needed to go to the airport in Omaha."

In the afternoon I received an email from Sonia requesting my presence. I knocked on her office door and heard an exuberant voice bid me enter. I half expected to see the professor with her little but big brother standing next to her, twirling a set of handcuffs, but instead she was alone.

Unlike Langstrom's den, Sonia's office breathed orderliness and cleanliness. Her books, standing neatly on an oaken bookcase, were not arranged by size, but they were, I noted, in alphabetical order, dustless, and no doubt bereft of dog-eared pages, and perhaps unread. Her desk, facing a wall, matched the bookcase in style, but on the wall, aside the monitor, hung a splendid mirror, which allowed the one sitting at the desk to not only check her makeup but also see who entered. It was in the mirror that her eyes met mine.

In a play, she would have made a believable

Elizabeth I, in real life she better resembled the Virgin Queen's half-sister, the one made of Vodka and tomato juice. She swiveled slowly around and with a gesture of the hand indicated the chair I was to occupy.

I sat down, my hands folded in my lap.

"Well, now," she began with a soft voice. "What have we found out about my dear Henry?"

"That he doesn't tape his password to his computer."

She laughed lightly and smiled as she retrieved her phone from her desk and flipped through her album of pictures. "Oh look at this one, you're very cute."

I didn't want to disagree with her, but I thought I looked rather uncomfortable sitting up in her bed.

"And then there's this one, but you left too early to be in it."

The picture was of her brother, whose mother obviously had mistaken steroids for Pablum when teaching him to eat from a spoon.

"Did you say Obelix was his name?" I wondered.

"Oh," she said, "here's another one with him taking fingerprints from my computer. Boy, was he upset when they didn't match my own."

"Your cleaning lady's, perhaps?"

"It appears you had my password, and I think I know how you got it." She set her phone on the desk and stared at it for a few seconds. There was something in her eyes that betrayed annoyance or perhaps concern or even fear. I can't say what exactly, but her attitude shifted from honeyed to hostile.

"If you're in cahoots with Tasia Everett you'd better drop the whole thing."

"Cahoots? With Tasia?" I was as dumbstruck as a cheerleader sent in to play middle linebacker.

"What has she threatened you with?" Sonia asked.

"Well," I said, reaching into the back of my mind to find something amongst the cluttered memories, "she did threaten to be friendly once, at least she put her hand on my forearm. Nothing came of it, sorry to say."

Sonia nodded slowly as if making up her mind about me. The outcome I believed was favorable because she took out a spoonful of honey and applied it to what she said next. "Deep down, I think you're a good young man, Tristan. You really don't belong in Langstrom's clique, and I would hope you would distance yourself from them as soon as you run through his computer files and find out his connection to Robert Jones. I'm giving you two-weeks' notice, and then you'll have to explain yourself to the sheriff."

"That sounds like a straight deal, and I thank you for your kindness, but couldn't you give me a hint about what I'm involved in? Just a clue as to what 'Robert Jones' stands for?"

"You know how people joke by saying, 'If I told you, I would have to kill you?'"

"Yes."

"Well, I wouldn't be joking."

"At least I'd die knowing why. I mean think of all the poor saps that wake up to a heart attack. No clue, just dead without explanation."

"Okay," she said, conceding. "Here's the deal: This office used to belong to your two chums, Henry and Al. They got along very well in here, but the dean decided that in order to avoid any legal action by the faculty union, each professor had to have his own office. So, the two conspirators were separated, sort of. I say sort of because they still meet together in Langstrom's office and spend their days together. I am surprised they don't team teach.

"Anyway, I get phone calls from time to time from people wanting to speak to Henry or Al. About a month ago, on a Tuesday, I got a call and it went to voicemail. Now, as you know, if you've got the same setup as I do, the generic prompt on my recorder saying 'I'm unavailable at the moment, please leave a message at the beep' is a male voice. Doesn't bother me because it causes most callers to just hang up because they think they dialed the wrong number. But on that Tuesday, it fooled whoever was calling in. The lady said, and I quote, 'I know who you are, you know who I am, Mr. History, and we both know who Robert Jones was.'" That's all the woman said, but it sounded threatening. So, I think there is or was something going on there between Henry and this Robert Jones, something no one wants aired in public. I suspect some emails might be more revealing, so that's your job. You provide me with info and I keep you out of trouble."

"And who is the lady?"

"That's a good question, and maybe you'll find me the answer. Whatever you do, though, don't mention Robert Jones to either Henry or Al. I don't want them to know I'm on to them. I'll save any damaging information, once I get it, for a key moment."

"Like for blackmail?"

"Let's just say that I think that if I get the goods on Robert Jones, I don't imagine anything could stop me from becoming Professor of the Year."

***

Back in the adjunct office, I meditated upon my plight. On the one hand, I felt pretty comfortable, having finished with the *Pax Romana* in class, I could steer clear of Bible origins for the rest of the semester. On the other hand, Sonia's request, or should I say, directive, did not sit well with me. And then there was the whole "Bible Study" enterprise, which had been a debacle. I mulled this over for a while and then decided I would bring the Bible study to a close come Thursday night. If I wanted to do something purposeful in life, such as work on my hermits, I needed to become an Epicurean and withdraw from all extraneous activities. I also needed to distance myself from Cambria.

On Thursday night our little group assembled once again at the Bookshire. Tasia was late, rushing in with a carry-on suitcase in tow.

"I'm sorry I'm a bit tardy. I just got back from visiting my grandmother. She's really not doing well."

Cambria looked at her luggage and asked,

"Where's she live?"

Tasia seemed surprised by the question. "In Minnesota," she started, then added, "...Michigan, rather, sorry. My other grandmother lives in Minnesota."

"You see how easily facts get mixed up," I commented before asking the more appropriate question, "Is there a chance she'll be improving, I hope?"

"I don't know," Tasia said with a genuine sadness in her voice.

"Michigan?" Cambria repeated.

"Yes," said Tasia, irritated.

"And the airline made you check your carry-on?"

Tasia looked at Cambria and then at her luggage. "Oh, yes...ugh, no. They took it at the airplane door, but they didn't check it. I didn't have to go to the baggage claim carousel to get it, anyway." She then turned to Franky. "Did you get my backpack to my room?"

He said he had it delivered, and she said she'd have to reward him for all that he had done for her. The awkward silence followed her proposal.

"Well," I finally said, "I've really enjoyed these Bible study nights, but we're going to break off our meetings for the future as midterms are upon us and because I'll have grading to do. And, after all, in class we're discussing the Roman Empire, and that covered the ministry of Jesus."

"You're just saying that," Cambria shot back at me, "because you don't want me bringing up Stephen."

"Stephen?"

"Yes, the first Christian martyred after Christ. Luke included him in his Book of Acts because he died like Christ, asking God to forgive his executioners. So, like I said, Luke would have definitely put Paul's martyrdom into his Book of Acts."

"Why do you get so worked up about this?" Tasia asked.

"Because if Luke wrote his Book of Acts before Paul was martyred, that means he wrote it in the early 60s AD, not the 80s. And that reveals something that would completely destroy Professor Telsmith's understanding of reality."

"How so?" I asked.

"If Luke wrote his Book of Acts in the 60s, it means that his first book, the Gospel of Luke, was written before Luke and Paul arrived at Rome."

Of course, her argument was complete

drivel, but I couldn't fathom why she thought Luke, or whoever wrote those two books, couldn't have written both in Rome. "You think Christians were forbidden to write in Rome?"

"No, but he couldn't have written his gospel in Rome because he said he got his information from eyewitnesses. He wouldn't go to Rome to get information about what Jesus did in Judea any more than you would go to Washington DC to get information about what Mayor Pilch accomplished in Aspinwall, Nebraska."

Then came a voice from the across the table. It belonged to the honor student, Angela. "So, when did he get the information and write his book?"

Cambria turned in her seat and softened her voice with hopes of luring the poor girl into her way of thinking. "There's only one period of time when Luke wasn't traveling about and was living in Judea where he would have had both the time and the opportunity to gather eyewitness information to write his gospel. It was from 57 to 60 AD, when his friend Paul was incarcerated in Caesarea, which was the seat of the Roman governor of Judea."

I felt obligated to point out that that was still three decades after the death of Jesus.

"Thirty years might seem like a long time to

us who are in our twenties," she riposted, "but if you ask my parents, well thirty years ago seems like yesterday, and so they reminisce about their college days as if they happened yesterday. And what they're telling me are firsthand stories. Thirty years is not enough time to be telling stories from one generation to the next. Heck, Luke could have even talked to Jesus' mother. She would have been in her seventies. Many people back then who managed to reach adulthood lived on into their 60s and 70s. The trick was to survive childhood, but none of the 500 disciples who saw Jesus resurrected were children."

"500?" I had to smile at this. "You get that number from one of the letters of the Apostle Paul. Since your type believe the Bible has no errors, I suppose it has to be exactly 500, but that's such a nice round number that it's laughable. It would be so hard to know how many people allegedly saw Jesus resurrected without having everybody stand in a lineup to be counted. And if you can't trust the number 500, then you can't trust anything else in the Bible."

Cambria was muscling up to give another retort, but I told her it was time to break up the Bible study, and I added, "if you don't want to look at the Bible scientifically, you need to go to a church."

***

The next day in class, October 9, Cambria kept silent. It was an appreciated first. I believe I might have even been inspired to say, in a totally secular way of thinking, mind you, "Thank God". In fact, there may have been a collective "Thank God" because everyone had had enough of her religious rants.

Her bit of lockjaw allowed me plenty of time to explain how the Emperor Constantine transformed Christianity into something very different from what it had been at the outset.

From time to time during my lecture, my eyes did wander off in her general direction. Not only was she silent but she never typed a word into her laptop or even jotted something down with pen to paper. Her chin pointed menacingly in my direction and her usually big bright eyes she compressed into narrow slits. Tight as they were, an enormous amount of enmity nonetheless radiated from them, and I was delighted.

Tasia, disregarding the well-established but unstated student rule, which dictates that wherever a student sits on the first day of class he or she is thereupon bound to sit until the final exam is completed, had moved across the room and away from Franky. Like Cambria, he too dallied in his notetaking and glanced repeatedly in Tasia's direction.

When class was over, I found myself in the hall behind Tasia who had been overtaken by Franky.

"It doesn't mean I'm your girlfriend," I heard her say.

He came back at her and asked, "How could you do this to me?"

"You go after Cambria now; she should be the next notch in your belt."

Having said this, she walked off smiling, looking back over her shoulder long enough to wave her fingers and say a "Toodle-oo."

As I walked past Franky, I heard him mumble something that sounded like "nasty witch."

11

As professors had finished administering midterms by Friday afternoon, I gauged that Aspinwall would be awash in alcohol and recreational drugs by nightfall, with a dozen or so frat houses and sororities and an equal number in the private sector hosting parties to the purpose.

I know it doesn't seem logical that a young scholar immersed in the study of the hermit should venture out into a college town on such a night, but I must tell you that my dissertation is a rather negative assessment of the monastic movement. I'm not one to put Simeon Stylites on a pedestal. To prove this, it is in my interest to walk in upon a party or two and spread my good charm and enhance my reputation by indulging in enough beers to make my walk back to the car half as straight and twice as long.

So, after awaiting the end of astronomical

twilight, like Lucy Westenra might have done when pondering a drink, I closed the door to the office and set off in the direction of the loudest music. Ultimately I found myself at Girard and Third Streets, in Barton's backyard where loudspeakers drowned out all normal conversation and obliged those of us who wished to be heard to shout in another's ear.

I pushed open the gate, which I had to lift off the ground to get it to open all the way, and I soon found a free ear on the person of Quinton.

"Are you alone?" I asked as an icebreaker.

"Alone? No, I came with another guy, but he's disappeared."

"Need a new gate," I observed, watching someone else struggling to get in.

Quinton looked at me askance for a moment, then said, "No, we're not together. You looking for someone?"

"You'll do."

"Nah, I'm straight. I'll go get Jeffrey, he's keen on you."

By the time I realized Quinton had mistaken the word "gate" for "date," he was already on his cupidian mission.

Jeffrey's a nice enough young man, very smart, very conscientious as a student, but visibly embracing the gay lifestyle. I'd had him in class, and he would linger after lecture to elaborate on issues discussed, always a pleasure to talk to. Otherwise, though, we walk on different sides of the street.

I was surprised to see Al at the party, wandering about with an empty glass and saluting me with it. Al and Sim traditionally had their own to-do with Henry on Midterm Party Night, but Al soon informed me that Henry was taking the night off so he could get up early and pedal off on a *randonnée*. He owns a Decathlon mountain bike, and I don't know why. Aspinwall is hilly, but Henry normally rides down to the bike path, where he heads north up through Brownville and all the way to Nebraska City and back. The trail is as flat as the Missouri Valley.

I understand biking to go a short distance—say, from point A, home, to point B, work—but I don't quite understand the whole point of Langstrom's pointless six-hour round trip. One can get the same mileage in a sixth of the time by stepping on a gas pedal. As a bonus, one can also bring back a carload of groceries from Nebraska City. On a bike one can hardly manage a bottle of water, and by the time you're back, the water's drunk and gone.

It was as I contemplated this that we witnessed Tasia walking into the party. One of the several yard lights hanging about the perimeter caught her face just as she moved through the gate. She immediately stopped and stood there, poised, very much alive to the fact that she had become the center of attention and attraction. I don't think even Al manning the stage lights at the theater could have done a better job at highlighting beauty.

She simply outclassed every female present. Perhaps it was her dress. It was out of season, even if that night were unusually warm for October. The dress itself was nearly a formal, light blue in color, which made her forever tanned skin stand out in the light, and her décolletage was undoubtedly the envy of every female who'd applied for a job at Hooters and been rejected. Her face was flawless, no doubt due to meticulously applied make-up, including a dark lipstick that made her teeth shine, perhaps twinkle under the lamplight. The only wrinkle in her appearance was the purse hanging off her shoulder. It's hard to imagine Marilyn Monroe sporting a purse, or anything at all for that matter.

"She's hot!" I heard Barton shout into Franky's ear. In fact, due to a pause in the music, as the loudspeaker shifted from one song to another, everybody heard the assessment.

The musical silence was long enough for her to give a "Thank you, Barton."

Franky, however, glared at Barton, but I don't believe Barton picked up on that fact, as he was too busy giving Tasia the once over, and several times in a row. Tasia seemed drawn by this attention and sidled up against Barton. What she told him I couldn't hear as the music once again overtook all meaningful conversation.

A few students I'd had in class the previous semester wandered by and chatted with me. With the music our discourse was much like listening to someone talking through a faulty microphone. Very irritating. I wished I had read the sports page a little more attentively, then I could have done all the talking.

By ten thirty or so, someone had the brilliant idea of turning down the volume.

Al happened by again about this time. By the looks of him he'd emptied one of Barton's kegs. He said a few things. One might have thought that with the music turned down I would have understood him, but that would be to discount the eloquence of the drunk.

He soon made a path for another keg just tapped to get a refill; however, with his eyes more on Tasia than where he was going, it took him some time before he topped off his glass.

"Despicable!"

I turned to see who had hollered this "Despicable" into my ear.

I was surprised. "I didn't think you religious types, apart from Tasia's boyfriend Franky, frequented these dens of iniquity."

Cambria was wearing her narrow eyes, but this time they weren't aimed at me. "Even Christ ate with publicans and prostitutes," she shouted out of the side of her mouth.

I edged away from the loudspeakers, but mostly to get away from Cambria. Regrettably, she followed.

"I don't remember her asking for any money," I said of Tasia, "and I don't remember Christ calling prostitutes 'despicable'. In fact, if he called anybody despicable, it was the religious leaders."

"I thought you didn't believe in anything the New Testament said."

"Well, I'm trying to be sociable by speaking your language."

"You know the truth."

"In a Socratic way, I suppose."

"What's that supposed to mean?"

"Socrates, unlike all the other wise men of Athens, knew that he didn't know, and hence was the wisest of them all."

"Everyone knows there's a God. You sense it as soon as you can think. Little children accept it easily. Not because it's childish, but because it's logical that there's a Creator. Then most spend the rest of their lives trying to destroy that childhood knowledge. Maybe even Socrates did."

"Oh, no. His last request was a gift to the god of healing. Besides, why would anyone who's tricked himself into believing that God exists want to destroy his belief in God? I mean it must be a wonderful crutch."

"It's no crutch to admit there's an omnipotent God. The real crutch is to camouflage your knowledge of God, so you can live the easy, selfish life. So you don't have to do what God would have you to do."

"Like love your enemies. Isn't that what Christ is supposed to have said?"

"No other religion teaches it. And for a reason: you can't do it unless you let Jesus into your heart, which means you have to repent of your rebellion against God, repent for saying that you don't believe in him."

"Do you love Tasia?"

"It's hard to. That's where God takes over."

"I heard Franky call her a witch. What does

the Bible tell you to do with witches? And, for that matter, what does the Bible have to say about gay people? You love them too?"

"You're gay?"

"Not at all. Why do you ask?"

For the first time I saw Cambria blush. I'll admit it was dark, but the way she looked down and away with her eyes, there had to be a pinkening of the cheeks. I was, to say the least, confused by this behavior. Maybe she had a different side to her, I thought.

"You want to take a little walk?" I wanted to test the waters to see if she had any feelings my way. If she did, I had a plan.

"Where to?"

"Just around. This party's too noisy."

She hesitated.

"I'll give you a good thirty seconds' head start," I told her. "You walk out the gate and then I'll dally about and come out later and no one will suspect a thing. We wouldn't want anyone to think we were on friendly terms."

She smiled and then made for the gate.

And I was true to my word and found her waiting on the sidewalk.

***

Campus Menace

We walked north, down Girard Street, toward the river. On either side were houses thrown together from different eras. A brick two-story dating back to the 1870s. On its facade was a portico with columns. The manse looked down upon its neighbor across the street, a low, one-story, wood-framed structure with a wooden porch whose posts, viewed straight on, had an angular trapezoid look. The latter was no doubt a 1920s Montgomery Ward bungalow that had looked spiffy and modern in its day but now seemed self-consciously mediocre and out-of-date. Other structures fell in between these two extremes and the ensemble gave one a sense of freedom, of creativity, as if one might be able to build any house of one's choosing. The atmosphere suited my purposes.

My plan was to appear amicable so that the grief I caused Cambria by striking the death knell for the Bible study might be assuaged. It would be hard for her to start up another vitriolic assault upon me during class if I had proven to be, in the end, a good-natured and generally chipper fellow. Judas aside, what student has the audacity to strike down a teacher who has taken her into his confidence, walked down from the mount with her, side by side, to the Jordan's edge, and forgiven her of her sins?

I asked Cambria about family, siblings, and pets. From the sound of it, she had a happy childhood but seemed to have lost privileges at times for talking back. I tried to look surprised.

The pet is always a good topic to broach when trying to win over another's sympathy, because everyone has possessed, at least once in his life, the smartest or most singular cat or dog. Even Sonia Abbot waxed about her Pekinese, Spot. Why one would name a Pekinese "Spot" I'll never know. With a Dalmatian it obviously goes without saying, but a fluffy whitish duster hasn't the least claim on the name. The little rag must have been embarrassed to no end. Perhaps that's why it ran under the wheel of Langstrom's Lincoln Navigator.

By this time we had turned left and were on Levee Road. This area of town was once dominated by warehouses connected to the dock just beyond the levee. The river traffic died away after World War II, especially after the erection of the Langdon Bridge, which spans the river just beyond the car wash. Of course, once semi-trucks began delivering goods directly to stores, the large warehouse buildings were torn down and ranch houses replaced them.

While passing the car wash, Cambria was

telling me the usual stories one hears from people about their dog: How it could understand the words "cookie" and "outside," but never could understand "don't bite the UPS man." Then she turned the tables on me and asked if I had had any pets.

I soon had her laughing about my dog Quetzalcoatl, or 'Quetzy' as we called her. Well, the story wasn't exactly about Quetzy but about her evening meal. I had been out mowing the lawn one late summer afternoon, like every suburban boy of fifteen ought to be doing when not reading a book, and having finished my chore, I came in for a glass of iced tea. It was near supper time and I found the tea in the fridge and sat down at the table. Laying there in plain sight was a casserole of sorts, piled high on a plate, that my caring mother had placed there to feed the hungry. I put the whole contents down the hatch while Quetzy, a sorrowful looking beagle, gazed at me imploringly with pleading whimpers. I may be a compassionate person, but when it comes to food for an adolescent who, through diligent feasting, is putting on the only muscle he'll ever have, I knew where to draw the line. I told the dog as much with a growl.

It was then that Mother arrived to tell me

that Quetzy should not be growled at too harshly as it was her food after all. She explained that she had taken all the out-of-date leftovers and heaped them onto a plate that was intended exclusively for the canine of the family. Part of my evening, therefore, was spent on all fours, much like a dog, on the bathroom floor whilst my stomach attempted, again much like a dog, to regurgitate the day's feeding. Quetzy stood faithfully beside me, coaching me I believe, but myself, not being a dog, failed in my attempt and the balance of the evening was spent in the ER.

I don't know why Cambria took this story to be so amusing. Probably because I had been in such pain with the lower intestine, as I explained, trying to inflate itself by gaseous means into a football. At least that's the way I felt it.

Speaking of dogs, I should add that once we reached Levee Road, we turned left to come back up Lawrence Street. Normally when I pass by Langstrom's house his dog, a German Shepherd, lets out three wild barks and then stops. This time he picked up on the scent of my companion and barked incessantly, obviously trying to warn me of something. We males, of whatever species, do stick together.

The subject of dogs eventually and naturally led us to speak of British TV and in particular their detective series. Whenever a dog shows up, in one of those mysteries, out for the casual walk with the master in some timbered space, you know a body is soon to be discovered. We agreed that it happens more than once in *Midsomer Murders*. And having arrived at the title of that show, we finally found a topic outside of family and family pets that connected us.

I've never met anyone before who could attach an episode title to an episode number, but Cambria possesses the gift. You just blurt out episode 14 and she says "Garden of Death." Of course, the fact that I could blurt out "episode 14" and then say that she was right in saying "Garden of Death" means that I'm just as much a Midsomer nerd as she.

Approaching the garden gate at Barton's, I believe I puffed out my chest an inch and nearly took off my Clark Kent glasses. There were grounds for being proud. I had completely flipped the enemy. At one moment she despised me, and now, at another, she enjoyed my company.

Naturally I had no intention of keeping company with her once we parted ways at

Barton's. She was a horrible person. Even as a child. It was proven by her confessions. Opinionated, insolent, and a host of other adjectives I could give you if I had a thesaurus in hand.

But I was happy we would be parting ways on good terms, at least from her perspective. I could henceforth teach at peace and spend more time with my hermits. And I could tell by the timbre of her voice as we reached the gate that nothing now could lessen her esteem for me, for I was a good hearted, caring, gentleman kind of guy. The type she could date even, although it would have to be to some sort of Billy Graham type event. As I looked at her now glowing, glistening eyes in that same lamplight that had once spotlighted Tasia, I thought I could even see wedding bells swinging in them.

Opening the defective gate for us was Quinton with a friend at his side, hand on his hip and a winning smile.

"I heard you were looking for me," said Jeffrey hopefully.

***

Cambria looked at the two of us, finishing with a glance thrown my way. It was a glance that transmitted a full-featured film teeming with meaning. In it I saw anger and disgust.

The anger made it evident that the disgust was not because she believed I was gay, which I was not, but rather because she thought she had been lied to, misled; that I had toyed with her emotions.

I myself had mixed emotions. On the one hand, all my effort to charm her had now come to naught; but on the other hand, it was a pleasure to see her displeased, outraged. Of course, the dragonfly in the ointment (a simple fly won't do) is that she would be on the prowl again, seeking to ambush me from the front row during lecture. Clearly on the horizon was the old WSE, the woman scorned effect.

Jeffrey was more of an immediate problem. He wanted to talk hermits, which is my Achilles heel. Our immersion into the subject drove Quinton away, which may have been Jeffrey's objective.

Al finally saved the night by asking me to drive him home. Jeffrey reasonably mentioned that the professor's house was easily within walking distance and there were still many hermits to discuss. Al countered that hermits could be fully discussed on any night of the week, or even during daylight hours, but that he had to be getting on soon, otherwise he would lose all the beer he had consumed before reaching home station.

"Besides," he added with a burp, "there's no way I can make it home afoot. It seems I've lost the north, or rather it's lost me. It keeps spinning about, changing direction. Under these uncertain conditions, I wouldn't make it home until dawn."

"I can point you in the right direction," offered Jeffrey.

"Nope, I need someone like Tristan here." He eyed me unsteadily. "It is Tristan, isn't it?"

"Yes," I said.

"And you know where the north is don't you?"

I confessed I did.

"That settles it," said Al in nodding. "You can drive me home, no need to walk the distance arm-in-arm, except to get me up to the front door once we arrive. And you know which way to turn the doorknob, don't you?"

"It's one of those you turn leftwise, right?"

"Now, don't confuse me."

I told Al it would take but ten minutes to go get my car, then I bid adieu to Jeffrey and jogged up to the campus and returned with the Batteredmobile, which is a black Impala that, other than its color, looks very little like the famed Batmobile. Stanley is the one who christened it the "Batteredmobile," and simply because it has a crease in its hood. You know how picky Stanley is about appearances.

The crease, I should say, came from a slight forgetfulness on my part. I was heading up Highway 75, in the stretch before the airport where 70 miles an hour is allowed, when I asked myself whether I had latched the hood or no. The answer immediately came back to me from the hood itself as it flew up against my windshield. This left me guessing as to my trajectory. Given that the highway is fairly straight, I felt that I had little to fear, but as I came to a stop by impacting a berm off the right side of the road, I understood that though the highway was straight, the steering wheel had a mind of its own. Anyway, the berm cracked and loosened my bumper and tweaked the orientation of my headlights, and the wind had bent and rattled the hood sufficiently so that, given its ripples, it now shuts at an angle. Otherwise, no real harm done.

So, having easily identified my Batteredmobile in the parking lot, I settled myself behind the wheel, sped away, reporting back, "Bang-Pow-Zap!!!" to the party. Arriving,

I aimed my lights as best I could at the man at curb's edge, whose upper body swayed back and forth like an air dancer.

"Is that you in your car?" Al asked with a squint and a slur.

I got out, like an efficient EMT, hustled my patient into the passenger seat and then sped away. All I lacked was a siren and flashing lights.

"My God," he said. And then he repeated this six or seven times as if doing it as an act of penance. Finally, he went into a little soliloquy that people in drama are famous for. Minus the burps and slurs, it ran something like this: "Barton was right, she's a hot one. Old Sim has her in International Relations. She'd be good at international relations. A perfect liaison officer. I should know."

Then he turned toward me with his head wobbling and his finger pointing, or rather waving at my nose, and declared, "Old Simmy's a sneaky one."

Once at curbside, I escorted Al's unstable body up to the door, turned the doorknob and bid him goodnight. Returning to the car, I played with the radio until I'd tuned into the Nebraska City station. It wasn't for the music but rather for the sports updates. With the

World Series looming and local football teams stomping about the gridiron, it's always best to keep abreast; such information, along with rainfall and grain yields, is the bread and butter of starting conversations in the cornhusker state. Sometimes, that's all you have time to talk about. I don't know what they do out in California where it doesn't rain for four months straight. They must have short conversations.

Anyway, putting the car in gear, I instinctively looked over at Al's house, perhaps to make sure he was all right. A light came on inside. Through the bay window I could see him enter the living room, look at his watch, pick up a book from the side table, then toss it on the coffee table, before disappearing into the kitchen. As I pulled forward, he reappeared in the living room with a bottle of water. Evian by the look of it. One has to admire the drunk who can drink half a keg and yet be thirsty.

I smiled, honked, and waved. He hesitated, leaned forward, whether intentionally or inspired by the muse of drink, then raised the bottle at me in a 'Here's-to-ya' fashion.

My journey north to Brownville ought to have been a pleasant one, but I had an odd feeling I couldn't quite define. Mixed sentiments about Tasia? Or was it Cambria? Or was it what

Al said about Sim? Or was it about Al having drunk so much? I couldn't decide.

***

That Friday, October 9, marked the beginning of Fall Break. Today is Sunday, October 18th, the end of Fall Break. In between the two dates I spent a day or two correcting midterms, but the rest of the time, to the sorrow of my hermits, I've spent writing down what you've just read, all the way up to dropping off Al, recalling the whole semester to mind and in particular the actions of Cambria and Tasia.

Now that a week has passed, it's evident that something is amiss. Tasia has yet to surface. Last time seen, walking from the Bookshire up toward the dorm. What could have happened to her? Is the answer found in the recitation of events that I have just given you?

I feel that it is, even in the tedious debates we've had about religious topics. And since, in the end, historians are but unglorified detectives, sorting out answers to riddles of the past, it is, I find, my duty to solve the Bookshire mystery.

But rather than give you daily reports dribbling out as droplets from a leaky faucet, I'll set aside my pen until the matter is resolved, and I can give you an uninterrupted stream of information.

12

I'm happy to report that the mystery has been solved, and solved not long after the end of fall break, so I return to the keyboard to fill in all the details.

When classes resumed on Monday, October 19, it was evident that Tasia, known for roaming from seat to seat in my classroom, had roamed away definitively, and I couldn't wait to get started trying to find out what had happened to her. So, when I had finished my lecture, in spite of the coldness that had arisen between Cambria and me, I invited her to stick around after class.

She may have been curious about what I had to say to her, but she didn't betray it.

"Any news concerning Tasia?" I asked warmly.

She answered coolly, "I didn't think you would care."

"Oh, but you underestimate me," I said, "I do care, and not just for the intellectual challenge of unraveling a mystery. If I begin losing students one by one, I'll be out of a job come January."

"I hear they hire adjuncts down at Stickers."

"Even so, there will still be the mystery gnawing away at me while I spike your drinks."

"There is no mystery, apparently."

"No mystery?"

"Jennifer, her roommate, says she received a postcard from Tasia on Wednesday."

"A postcard?"

"That's why I say apparently. Who sends postcards these days, except grandmothers?"

"Yes, you would think an email or a text message would do. Think of the effort it would be for someone of Tasia's disposition to write out a message in longhand. However, typing just might break a nail. Risks everywhere."

We didn't say anything for a minute. At first, I thought Cambria was impatient to leave, but then, on second thought, I saw disappointment or sadness in her. She had a crestfallen look.

"Anyway," I said to revive the conversation, "what did Tasia say in her postcard?"

"She said she'd had it with college and wouldn't be back, except to pick up her clothes and things some day."

"Strange, I didn't know she was putting all that much effort into her classes. Did she elaborate? Say where she was going? Back home maybe?"

"No, just 'I've had it with college and I'm not coming back. Love to all, Tasia.'"

"She included me in that love?" I asked hopefully. Cambria didn't answer, so I offered another question: "Are they sure the postcard was from Tasia?"

"Jennifer said it looked like her handwriting and from what I understand, the police compared the fingerprints on the card with those found in her dorm room, and they matched."

"They didn't have her fingerprints on file, as they say in the movies?" I was really saying this to myself, but I'd also said it out loud. It seemed important somehow.

Up to this point, Cambria had spoken with a subdued, why-am-I-bothering-to-tell-you-all-this attitude. But the way I asked this question caught her attention. "Are you sincerely interested in what happened to Tasia?"

"Like I said, yes...I have no ambition to spike your drink."

At that moment students started trooping in

for the next class session.

She looked at her phone. "I've got chemistry, how about we meet at the Bookshire in two hours?"

I told her I'd rather meet in the evening at Stickers, then we could have dinner. She looked a bit oddly at me when I offered this. That is to say she smiled uneasily, so I made it clear I wasn't making a date of it.

"No, I wouldn't expect that of you." She looked a bit crestfallen again.

"Okay," I said, to resurrect her spirits. "The Bookshire it is. Six p.m."

Crested or not, she arrived at the Bookshire sooner than I, and when I entered, she hailed me like a street cop pulling someone over.

She was on the coffee shop side of the establishment, sitting at a table at the far end, lodged between the facade's window counter and an empty booth.

I approached her table and she patted the chair next to her. I took the hint and sat down.

"You're sincerely willing to help me find out what happened to Tasia?" she asked.

"As long as you don't think every clue we find leads to something confirming the authenticity of the New Testament."

Her brow darkened as she pondered this

condition. "Okay, I won't bring up the Bible or your nonsensical ideas about it unless you, or someone else, bring it up first."

I agreed to the proposal.

"Listen," she then said quietly but energetically, "why wouldn't they have her fingerprints 'on file'?"

"Well," I answered, "if she had committed no crime, she may never have had anyone ever take her fingerprints."

"Still, why would she send a postcard? That's something some old biddy or someone like me would do. And if she did, why wouldn't she explain things in it? Something's fishy. I think she's dead!" She crossed her arms and gave a sharp bob of the head to emphasize the point.

"Dead?"

"M-u-r-d-e-r-e-d," she spelled out.

"Why would anyone kill her?"

She bobbed her head back again, arms still crossed, as if I was a moron for asking the question.

"Listen, Cambria, the only way to know who could have harmed her, if anyone, is to find out where everyone was and what they were doing on the night she disappeared. That's rule number one in *Midsomer Murders*."

Cambria dug into her backpack and brought out her laptop and switched it on. "Okay," she said. "Can Jeffrey account for where you were all Friday night and Saturday morning?"

"I doubt it, I got rid of him fairly fast."

"I take it that you didn't take him home with you?"

Now I was crossing my arms. "Is this a murder inquiry or a let's-find-out-about-the-professor's-personal-life inquiry?"

"Both."

"I'm not gay."

Cambria let out a breath of air like a punctured inner tube. It sounded like a sound of relief. "Okay," she said. "What did you do then?"

I recounted, in detail, my mission to get Al back home in the upright position and my drive back to Brownville. "And Stanley can verify when I came back, he was there, serving me whiskeys until we both began to talk and walk like Al."

"Yes," she said chewing on her lower lip, "we would have to get Professor Tate to confirm the time you dropped him off, though." She tilted her head like Joan of Arc listening for those angelic voices. After a moment she said, "Run that part back to me again, where you dropped off Professor Tate."

I recounted again how I had taken him to the door and then watched him through the bay window for a minute or two before leaving. I included every detail I could remember.

"Very interesting," she remarked as she typed what I had said into a Word document. "Yes indeed, I believe we should go have a visit with Professor Tate."

"Why?"

"Because there's something that's been bothering me. I heard from a student that he didn't have class because Professor Tate went to Boston to see his publisher."

"True, but what does that tell us?"

"Nothing by itself, but I noticed that when Tasia came to Bible study with her carry-on, it had been checked through to Logan Airport, which is in Boston."

"She said it hadn't been checked."

"Well I didn't believe her, so I followed her, and she ripped off the tag as soon as she thought she wasn't being watched, crumpled it up, and threw it into the gutter."

"And you picked it up out of the gutter."

"You bet. Her bag had been checked. So why was she lying to us?"

"So, you're saying they both went to Boston. That is a coincidence."

"On the same day! And that's not a coincidence. Those two had a rendezvous that they didn't want anyone to know about."

"Hmmm," I said as I thought back to something Al had said. "I don't want to say too much ill of Al, he's generally a good sort, but you do make me wonder. He said Tasia would make, and I quote, 'a perfect liaison officer, and I should know.' I thought that in his drunken stupor he was suggesting she be a liaison officer to high school teachers."

"Why? What is a liaison officer?"

"Well, that's what he and Langstrom were in college. They worked with high school faculty to encourage high-schoolers to become history majors and participate in certain competitions that had to do with history. I thought Al was just being funny, suggesting that Tasia, being the sex-bomb she is, would recruit a lot of students. Now, however, judging from his words 'I should know,' maybe he meant something quite different."

"You mean like he's had an affair with Tasia?"

"Perhaps, but I don't want to think that of him. Besides, it would be hard to prove that he had an affair with Tasia, and it would be even harder to prove that an affair has anything to do with Tasia's disappearance. It wouldn't be the first time a student and a professor developed an amorous relationship. Unethical if the student is in his class. He wouldn't be awarded Professor of the Year, that's for sure."

"Well, then," said Cambria, "if we want some clarity, there's only one thing to do."

"And that is?"

"What I said before, we must go see Professor Alfred Tate."

I had no objection. Al was a very welcoming sort of man who appreciated clarity, and not being one to own a flowerpot, his front door was always unlocked for the visiting public. Even his garage was usually left wide open, and I'm not sure he didn't leave his SUV unlocked, and with the keys in the ignition.

We arrived at Tate's house on Holiday Street at eight p.m. As we stepped out of the Batteredmobile and then onto the porch, we could hear jazz playing in the background. I don't quite understand jazz, especially when there's some throaty woman singer trying to seduce you with a voice three octaves lower than your own.

We stood there for a moment, staring at the door.

"Shall we knock?" asked Cambria.

"I don't think it would do a bit of good," I told her, thinking of the music. I opened the door and managed to override the singer's voice with an "Al? You home?"

"Yes, yes, I'm here. Come on in Tristan," Al called out as he dimmed the singer's voice a notch with the remote and approached us. "What brings you round?"

"Well, Cambria and I were trying to figure out what happened to one of her classmates, Tasia Everett. Cambria and Tasia are in my Western Civ class."

"Yes, I've heard of Tasia's leaving the college." Looking the two of us over, it dawned on him who Cambria was. "And I've heard of you as well, Cambria. I understand you're quite the Biblicist."

It instantly came to me that I should have called Al first before coming, so I could have warned him against using Bible-related words within earshot of my Watson.

"I'm sure I know less than Professor Telsmith, but what I do know is true."

"And what would that be?" asked Al, taking the bait and swallowing it.

"That Constantine did not invent Christianity three hundred years after Jesus died on the cross."

"Have a seat," suggested Al as he plumped himself down into an armchair.

In front of him was a small glass-topped coffee table with an ottoman beside it, and beyond these was a couch, the size of a love seat. He unfortunately pointed to it.

Cambria sat down first and, rather surprisingly, put her feet on the ottoman.

Maybe to send the message that she was at ease and wasn't going to be intimidated. I believe she can be subconsciously theatrical in that way. I reluctantly squeezed in next to her.

"You know I'm not all drama," he said, "I did a master's in history, which is why I, too, am a venerable member of The Social Sciences Club. And as I recall those classes relevant to the subject, I would say the Christians had lots of ways of conceiving of God before Constantine declared there was only one way, his way. A God in three persons. To wit: Father, Son, and Holy Spirit. A Trinity, *n'est-ce pas*? Why, according to one Christian leader of the day, Arius by name, Jesus was only a secondary god, not the real God."

"Recognizing that God exists in three persons," Cambria shot back, "is the only way the New Testament makes sense if you want to remain true to Judaism."

"Judaism?"

"Jesus' disciples were Jews, monotheists, and yet they believed Jesus defined himself as the 'I Am', which was the name God gave himself in the Old Testament. They couldn't have Jesus as a second god. It's nonsense."

"As I recall, it was Constantine who organized and presided over the Nicene Council that forbade Christians to refer to Jesus as a secondary god."

"The Trinity isn't something Constantine came up with any more than a farmer concocts a chemical formula for an herbicide. Constantine wasn't a theologian."

"Somebody came up with it."

"Yes, the bishops of the Empire did, and they were just echoing what had been said before, in the New Testament and by their predecessors. Arius is the one who invented a new theology."

Cambria paused to take her breath, which was never a good sign. Al sat there, mouth open in imitation of a Missouri catfish.

"Well," she said reeling him in for the kill, "maybe Arius wasn't all that creative. He was teaching the same thing you find in pagan philosophy back then, Neoplatonism. A pure God and then a lesser god, a guide to lead you to the purely spiritual Deity. Arius's teaching was just pagan philosophy refitted with a Christian-sounding vocabulary—"

"Uhummm," I uttered, breaking off Cambria's lecture. "Arianism aside, we were wondering if you had any ideas about Tasia's disappearance."

Like others before him, myself included, Al projected a sigh of relief in escaping the

Cambrian juggernaut, not unlike the "Ahhh" of a fifteen-year old whose football-sized intestine suddenly shrinks to normalcy.

"Ahhh, that," he said. "I have no idea. I remember she was at that party. Yes, Cinderella entering the ballroom," he recalled, reminiscing with his head down and his eyes fixated on Cambria's black leather pumps with stout heels.

Then he looked up at us. "You know, I was thinking of doing a Cinderella play. If she comes back, I'll track her down. And you, Cambria, have you ever been a stepsister?"

Cambria, in one of those rare moments that you wish were an endless ball of string so you could stretch it out ad infinitum, was at a loss for words.

"Hmm," he said studiously as he observed her more closely. "I'm also planning a play entitled *The Bewitched* for next summer, it's one I've written. It promises to be a big hit, considering the advance from my publisher. You wouldn't mind trying out for the part of Mariana of Austria, would you?"

"What's it about?" Cambria gleefully asked.

"It's a story about Charles II, the last Habsburg of Spain. The mother, Mariana, has an excellent role in it."

"I've never been in a play before, but it's

flattering for you to ask."

"Yes, yes. I'll keep you in mind," Al said. "But meanwhile, what about Tasia?"

"We're concerned about her," I said. "Maybe she's in danger, or worse. We want to find out what happened to her. When was the last time you saw her?"

"Oh," he said, leaning back and crossing his arms. "Foul play, you think? Well, last time I saw her was at the party. She was with—"

"Why did you drink water?" Cambria interrupted.

"What?"

"When you came home from the party, Professor Telsmith said he saw you go into the kitchen, grab a bottle of water, and drink it."

"Oh, well, I must have been fairly smashed because I don't remember Tristan being with me. But if you say so."

"No, he saw you from his car, through your bay window. You walked across the living room, tossing a book on this table," she said pointing at the coffee table with a nod, "and then you walked into the kitchen where you got a bottle of water and drank it."

Al looked over at me.

"I wasn't spying on you," I said defensively. "I just noticed. I'm the one who dropped you off.

I don't know why she's asking about the water." I looked at Cambria reproachfully.

She ignored me and came back at him. "Why did you drink water?"

"You need to drink more beer and read less Bible. But for future reference, if you've got a belly full of beer and don't drink a lot of water before turning in, you'll wake up in the middle of the night thirsty and with a headache. Well, to be quite honest, you may wake up a little thirsty and with a bit of a hangover anyway, but it won't be as bad as it could be."

"So, you walked right through here, tossing this book onto the table, and into the kitchen, where you grabbed a bottle of water, before coming back out here to sit down and read the book." Cambria hedged on the idea that he sat down to read. I had driven off with him sucking on the bottle.

"I suppose so, if Tristan saw me do so."

"And then what time did you go to bed?"

I came to Al's rescue. "I dropped you off sometime around eleven."

"Then there you have it. Between eleven and eleven thirty p.m., the time to drink a bottle of water and perhaps read a bit." Suddenly, Al sat up in his chair. "You know, this sounds like a spot of fun. Kind of being like detectives, isn't it? You mind if I take the part of Holmes, or even Watson?"

"Be our guest," I offered.

He thought a bit and then said, "You know that Barton was awfully friendly with Tasia, but I don't see how he would want any harm done to her. I think he rather likes her alive and pretty."

He paused in thought, then added, "You know, there was something strange that happened that night. It seems Sonia came home late, about midnight, if I'm not mistaken. Strange because I can't imagine her flitting off to student parties on Midterm Party Night and coming home late. Now if President Larimer or someone equally influential were sponsoring a shindig, then she would stay out until the host went to bed, maybe go with him; but there was nothing of the sort going on that night."

"How would you know what time she came home?" Cambria asked.

"I heard voices.... I was still not too clear-minded."

"So, like Joan of Arc?" I offered.

"No, real voices," he assured me. "She must have been on the porch talking to someone. I did hear her say one word loudly, like she was surprised, or perhaps she was insisting on something. Yes, yes. 'Crematorium,' that was it."

The idea that Sonia might be involved sparked my synapses. If only she could be a killer then all this bother about Robert Jones would be literally out of my way for life, assuming we got the conviction.

I began my round of questioning the witness. "Did Sonia do anything else unusual that night or the next day?"

"No, though she did have a man out back of her house digging up an area. Maybe for a garden next spring. I didn't pay much attention at the time. Just glimpsed the man's rear end from the upstairs window. He was bent over, you see. Looks like he was preparing a flower garden. He had set up a fountain in the middle of it."

"When was this?"

"I don't know, may have been done Sunday...or no, perhaps the day after the party, Saturday. Yes, Saturday morning because I was just out of bed, though rather late, and in my robe, and wondering what the consequences might be if I ate breakfast."

Cambria and I looked at each other simultaneously, just like any two people who had watched all hundred-and-fifty-odd episodes of *Midsomer Murders* would look at each other.

"You don't have a shovel, do you?" she

asked.

Al looked confused. He obviously hadn't seen enough *Midsomer Murders*.

"Suppose so," he admitted, but with a questioning voice. "In the garage, perhaps?"

His garage was attached to the north side of his house, and we accessed it through the kitchen door. Hanging on the wall were several implements, everything from a crowbar to a shovel. I grabbed the one we needed, and Cambria and I, with Al trailing cautiously behind, headed out of the garage, around the back of the house. When we reached the hedge, which disguised the fence line, on the south side of Al's yard, we judged we were directly opposite Sonia's backyard.

"Do you have a ladder?" I asked Al.

"Am I to assume you intend to climb over the hedge, enter Sonia's property, and dig up Tasia's body underneath that fountain?"

"Episode 14, 'Garden of Death,'" Cambria said.

"What?" Al exclaimed.

"Episode 14," I explained, "where Neil Dudgeon is Mr. Bolt, the rakish gardener hitting on all the women."

Cambria chimed in. "No one would have guessed he would reform himself and change his name to Midsomer's redoubtable Detective Inspector John Barnaby."

Al shook his head, said we were nuts, and that he was going back inside. He also mumbled something about not wanting to be accused of being a peeping Tom.

"Did you have a good time with Tasia!" Cambria called out after him.

He turned around with a bewildered look on his face.

"I said," Cambria repeated, "Did you have a good time with Tasia? In Boston?"

"What?" he asked, obviously surprised.

"Yes, you and Tasia in Boston. You met her there, we know all about it."

"When?" he asked. Then he said, "Well, 'when' never matters, because I never did. I went to Boston to meet with my publicist."

"But when you weren't in his office, were you having a treat with Tasia?"

"Why would she be in Boston?" He stepped back over to us. "Oh, I see. You think I had a tryst with the girl, then strangled her, and tossed her body into Boston harbor like it was a crate of tea. Then, Sonia happened by, retrieved the crate, shipped it home via UPS, and then buried it under a fountain."

"Could be," said Cambria, suddenly less sure

of herself.

"Are you in on this 'line of inquiry' too, Tristan?" he asked me.

"Not really, but I couldn't blame you if you did have a night out with her. It's just that Cambria discovered that Tasia went to Boston the same day you did."

"Well, then, our affair had to take place in front of the Starbucks counter in the airport, the one near security. We had to put two tables together first to give us room, however."

"You're saying you never left the airport?" asked Cambria meekly.

"Nope, didn't even see the harbor. Max came to see me with all the paperwork right there at Starbucks. You can ask Michelle, she's the one who made my Americano. Max Tobini is my publicist."

"No offense," I said, "but it seems odd to go all the way to Boston to sign papers. Couldn't you just do all that over the internet?"

"I'm old school. I like to thrash things out face to face with Max. We had to plan the speaking events that go along with the performances. There's a Boston troupe doing the play next summer, and they plan on touring the East Coast. Why would I waste time taxiing about Boston when Max will come to the airport, much simpler. Besides, I got to meet Michelle."

We were properly chastened.

Al shifted his eyes to the hedge and shook his head, then turning toward his house, said, "You two have fun."

No sooner had he departed than Cambria took on the voice of a drill sergeant. "Get down on all fours!"

If my mother had not been a prosecutor, I would have said, "You first!" or something equally caustic and manly. But my mother had trained me to obey the female voice without hesitation.

"Where were you from eleven fifty-three to eleven fifty-nine a.m.!" Mother had once barked at me in my tender years. My initial answer was, as I recall, "I don't know." It was a reasonable answer, because at four years of age, I had not yet mastered the clock, digital or otherwise. "Three or four minutes ago!" returned the prosecution. "Right before being called to lunch!" It seemed she couldn't end a sentence without an exclamation mark. Then she gave that military sounding order, something to the tune of, "Get your hands from behind your back and on the table, now!"

Indeed, it was very much the same voice

Cambria had employed. As a four-year old, I remembered hesitating. The prosecutor didn't, though, and she grabbed my arms tightly, like she wanted to take my blood pressure, which was rising. Then she swung my little mitts up in front of her eyes and scrutinized my two hands, each one clutching a crayon. "These crayons match, in color and consistency, the scribbling on the far wall of the kitchen!"

She then passed on a recommendation addressed to my father, who was a defense lawyer except when facing this particular prosecutor: "I recommend the accused not have any crayons for the extent of two weeks!" Being an intelligent man, he assented. I think it was the tightness with which my mother squeezed my arms that taught me to obey a woman's command, and it has stuck with me.

So, having instinctively massaged my arms upon receiving Cambria's orders, I assumed the position of an equine. I soon felt Cambria's pumps digging into my back as she poked her nose over the hedge. I tried to take it like a good recruit but when she got comfortable by settling her heels into my spine, I fear a high-pitched groan escaped my lips.

"Quiet," she said. "I'm only 120 pounds."

"It's not the weight, it's the shoes."

"Well I wouldn't be able to see over the hedge without them. Besides, I'd make a liar of my driver's license if I took them off."

"How tall are you?"

"Five-six."

"Without the shoes?"

"I always have my shoes on."

"Even when you go to bed?"

"I'm not standing up when I'm in bed."

Coming from the other side of the hedge, I heard a sliding door open and a gasp from Cambria; and then I felt the full weight of her knees slamming into my back when she dropped down. Somehow, 120 pounds felt more like 220. I wondered if she had been as honest about her weight on her driver's license as she had been about her height.

I didn't have time to let out an "ugh" until my stomach hit the sod beneath. Cambria was sprawled across my back for a moment, but then she rolled off and popped up onto her heels.

"Whew! She nearly saw me!" she exclaimed. She waited a bit, then added, "Did you hear me? She nearly saw me!"

I managed to turn over and sit up on my derriere with my arms propping me up as buttresses. Listening to my lungs flailing away, I felt like one of those fellows on the Tour de France who has just reached the summit of the Pyrenees.

"What are you doing?" she asked. "You sound like you're having a panic attack."

I rose to my feet slowly and put my hands on my knees, fearing another mountain peak. Finally, I managed to ask what she had seen.

"There's a fountain and dirt dug up all around it."

"Well that's what Al told us."

"Of course, he probably can see it from that window up there."

I followed her finger and saw Al's face peering out a second story window.

"Yes," I agreed. "We'll have to come back at night to see if there's anything more to it. We'll leave the shovel under the hedge."

Much later, the Batteredmobile slipped through the streets of Aspinwall and arrived quietly in front of Al's house at ten thirteen p.m. I had picked Cambria up at ten p.m. precisely. It was a very James Bond-ish operation. I brought the Batteredmobile into the back parking lot, behind the dorm. After I parked, Cambria came up from behind, keeping a low profile beneath the roof of the cars, opened the back door, and slid onto the backseat, laying down as she shut the door. No one could have told there was anyone else but myself leaving the campus.

On the way to Al's I told her I had managed to get ahold of Max Tobini who corroborated Al's story. He met him at Starbucks within thirty minutes of Al's arrival and saw him enter security to catch his return flight.

"He just offered you all that information? No questions asked?"

"Al's the one who gave me his phone

number. He told me I needed to verify his alibi if we were going to eliminate him from the suspects list."

"That's just what a guilty party would do."

"I did google his publishing house," I said glancing into the back seat, "and I did find that a Max Tobini works there and that his cell phone number matched the one Al gave me."

I saw that Cambria had dressed for the occasion, all in black. Myself, I had gone back to Brownville prior to our new sortie, but I got so tied up with Stanley, telling him about our plans, that I kept my day clothes: tennis shoes, jeans, and a buttoned-up checkered shirt.

However, I didn't get a really good look at Cambria until we parked and she got out and crossed in front of the headlights.

"Those look like pajamas," I observed after exiting the Batteredmobile.

"It worked for the Viet Cong."

I left the car unlocked, windows down, and engine running, just in case we needed to expedite our departure.

As we moved up the walkway to Al's house, we saw him through the bay window reading a book while listening to his jazz. It's a talent I don't possess. When I'm reading a book, I can't have dialogue in the background, even if it's a crooner. It's not that I stop reading and start listening, rather it's that I can't focus on what I'm reading, and I can't quite grasp the lyrics.

Walking in, we hailed our fair-weather co-conspirator and he gave up the book to greet us.

"So, you're going through with this?" he asked.

"The die is cast, the Rubicon passed," I confirmed.

"Seems silly to me, but I put two stepladders out there. You can climb one, lift the other one over and place it on the ground on the other side and then climb down it. Mind you, if you're caught, I know nothing. You stole those stepladders and the shovel from my garage after binding and gagging me. That'll be my story."

"I believe you," I said. Then, turning to Cambria I gave a nod to indicate that Operation Body Snatch was underway. All we really needed, of course, was a wisp of Tasia's hair that could be traced to her through DNA analysis. It's in more than one episode of *Midsomer Murders*.

Al remained in HQ while the commando team moved stealthily along the back of the house with our path colorfully lit by the basement windows dressed in faux stained glass. Reaching the end of the house we moved into the darkness bordering the hedge.

Taking charge, I told Cambria to wait on Al's side of the hedge until I'd reconnoitered the objective.

She, on the other hand, had already taken one step ladder and set it up. As she climbed it, she ordered me to hand her the other stepladder once she was high enough to see over the hedge. We went with this second plan, mainly because she had already reached the top of stepladder number one.

She struggled with stepladder two for a bit as she hoisted it over the shrubbery, but she finally freed it from the leafy branches and placed it on the ground opposite us. Proving to be an acrobat, she kept her left foot on stepladder number one while she lifted her right foot over the hedge and put it on stepladder number two, thereby straddling the hedge. I held stepladder number one firmly in place.

When Cambria pushed off to shift the rest of her weight onto stepladder number two, I realized we probably should have asked somebody to hold stepladder number two in place, but the only person I could think of was Sonia, and that wouldn't do. She would have asked about the shovel.

I didn't have much time to consider the

problem in detail because stepladder number two leaned precipitously away from stepladder number one and Cambria's straddle got correspondingly wider. I'm glad she was wearing pajamas because anything tighter would have precipitated her fall onto the hedge two or three seconds sooner. From my side I could see her left foot, which she had unwisely taken off of stepladder number one when she fell, sticking out of the hedge; above it a left forearm protruded, and its hand waved about wildly while grasping at leaves, or perhaps straws, if that's what people are searching for when all hope is lost. Luckily for the acrobat, the fence within the hedge had stopped her descent about five feet off the ground.

"I see you changed your shoes," I observed. "Sneakers are much more practical for negotiating a hedge."

I heard no response for a moment or two, and then came a high-pitched groan.

"Quiet," I said.

Eventually I saw a chin stick out of the hedge, followed by a button nose. "I'm okay, thanks for asking. I've got most of my right leg over the fence. If you could just push me up, I think I can fall over onto the other side."

I gave a good heave to her left thigh while

she pulled herself up by grabbing at the shrubbery. Suddenly she disappeared and then I heard a thud and another one of those groans.

"I'm coming over," I whispered through the hedge.

"Okay, bring the shovel."

"I'll just toss it over."

"No!" she let out.

"You forgot to whisper," I said reprovingly.

She recognized her mistake and lowered her voice. "Just hand it to me from the top of the ladder."

Studying stepladder number one for a minute, I decided to experiment and removed it from its parallel park and positioned it facing the hedge. When I got to the top of stepladder number one, I found Cambria, who had resurrected stepladder number two, at eyelevel. She took the shovel, descended, and graciously held stepladder number two while I crossed over. It was a good lesson in physics.

Once on the ground, I followed her over to the flowerbed and what she had earlier described as a fountain, which turned out to be more of a birdbath.

We stared at it a bit in the moonlight, then Cambria, no doubt realizing after the stepladder incident that I should be in the lead, handed me the shovel and suggested I start the digging once we'd moved the birdbath.

"You don't think you should pause and offer a prayer for Tasia before we exhume her body?" I asked.

"Don't be ridiculous. Protestants don't pray for the dead."

I laid down the shovel and with Cambria pushed at the birdbath. It wouldn't budge.

"There's no other choice," she said. "You'll have to dig from the side to get under it."

I began my labors while Cambria kept vigil.

The ground was soft, even muddy where water from the birdbath had splashed, and it didn't take many shovelfuls before I hit pay dirt by striking something hard that wasn't the birdbath's foundation. I got down on my hands and knees. I hesitated. Was it poor Tasia's skull? A tuft of hair was all that was needed, but what if the whole head emerged, smiling at me with one eyelid down as if in a wink? I shuddered.

"It's not Halloween yet, is it?" Cambria asked.

"I shouldn't think so, it's usually on the 31st."

"Then why is someone inside Dr. Abbot's house masquerading around as a sheriff?"

"Is he big, mean looking, and not smiling?"

"Yes."

"Then I would hazard to guess that it's Sonia's little brother, Sheriff Abbot. What's he doing?"

"Well I can't see him through the basement windows anymore." She stood on her tiptoes hoping to get a plunging view. "Nope, gone. But it is pretty nice down there. A bedroom from the looks of it. And since the other window is glazed, I imagine it has an attached bathroom as well."

"Still no sign of him?"

"Nope. Now wait a minute. It looks like he has made it out of the basement and is coming to the sliding door."

The door whisked open and we slid behind the birdbath and froze in place. The sheriff powered on a flashlight that had probably once been used as a searchlight in some now forgotten stalag that had a rummage sale after World War II. Its beam illuminated the far corner of the garden that was off to our right. It slowly began its clockwise sweep toward us, halting first upon a chaise lounge before moving on to the statue of a gnome.

Thinking quickly, I discarded the idea of imitating a garden gnome and grabbed a handful of mud and rubbed it into Cambria's face. Dark as it was, I could see her eyes glaring at me, as if generating a light of their own.

"The Viet Cong did this," I whispered.

She took a handful herself and slapped my face with it.

"Ouch!"

Suddenly the searchlight went berserk, crisscrossing wildly in search of B-29 bombers.

I winced and shoved my hands underneath the birdbath, gripping the object below and yanking so hard that the image of my sixth-grade tug-a-war with Alice Pitchner came to mind. This time, I vowed, I wasn't going to lose, and what an inspiration Alice proved to be. The "thing" gave way and I summersaulted backwards, a first, and I ended up on my feet with prize in hand. I tucked it under my arm like a football and immediately dashed for the garden gate to the left side of the yard, yelling to Cambria, "Come on! Follow me! Forget the stepladders we stole from Professor Alfred Tate!"

The sheriff seemed to have had the same idea and centered the spotlight on us as he ran. It appeared to me that he must have played linebacker for the Kansas City Chiefs because he was getting up a pretty good head of steam and threatened to outrun his searchlight. Cambria obviously came to the same conclusion because she passed me, but as she did, I executed the perfect hand off. Then, running interference, I grabbed stepladder number two as we happened by it, executed a pirouette, rarely seen on the gridiron, and flung it into the path of the linebacker. Cut the legs right out from under him and not a flag in sight. To be honest, it was hard to see anything in detail because his searchlight went out. Continuing toward the gate, which I assumed Cambria envisioned as a goal post, I saw her toss the football over it and then bound up and over herself. I don't know if one can legally score a touchdown that way, but it was a field goal at the very least. With a leap equal to hers, I joined her on the other side.

I hit the turf running and neither of us slowed down until we'd landed in the Batteredmobile. I shoved the old gal into drive and spun the tires for a good twenty yards before they took hold of the asphalt to jettison us forward Zap! Bang! Pow! at Mach speed.

***

As soon as we got out of town, we turned off down a graveled country road, parked, and doused the lights.

I turned to Cambria and announced, "We'll just sit here for fifteen minutes or so until everything calms down."

"Okay, but what do you think this thing is?"

I turned on the dome light and looked in her lap and saw that the football had transformed itself into a wooden box, the type retailers use to put a cheap wine in, and then sell it for the price of a Saint-Emilion.

"Open it up," I suggested.

Cambria clawed at the box for a bit. "I can't, it's screwed in on every side."

"All right," I said, "we'll sit here for a bit, then we'll make our way over to my house slowly, down the country roads. When we get there, we'll find a screwdriver and open it up."

Before I flicked off the dome light, Cambria told me to leave it on for a moment. She dug into her purse and pulled out a book, *Life in a Casket*.

"It's a cozy mystery about a woman who investigates crimes in Brownville in the 1850s," she explained. "I wanted to get started on it tonight. My mother says I'll be surprised to learn who the heroine is." She opened the book and stuck a little lamp atop it and pushed a button. "You can turn off your light now," she said.

The first page and her face both shone.

"Don't you think we should turn off all the lights," I said. "We don't need to attract attention."

"You really think we're going to attract attention on the back roads of Nemaha County. I don't think I know a single person in the whole of New York City who's even heard of Nemaha County."

"You've asked them?"

"How could I, I don't know any." Then she ignored me and began reading to herself.

Twenty pages later, I pulled into 215 South 6th Street and parked. Cambria, holding the box, followed me up the brick path. I unlocked the door and after getting through the entryway, we reached the kitchen. Sitting at the far end of the table and facing us was Dr. Sonia Abbot.

***

I may have looked slightly stunned for a moment, but I recovered quickly. "I was hoping you'd be here," I said. "We found something of yours."

"I like your make-up. Did you get it through Amazon or from the Amazon?"

"No, we got it locally, cheap as dirt."

"My brother tells me you're facing three months in jail and a five-hundred dollar fine. And that's just for trespassing. I'm sure assaulting a peace officer carries more serious penalties, but he's willing to settle that out of court. You may want to take a crash course in the martial arts."

"Nothing to do with me," I said, using the voice of my father, the defense lawyer, "I thought he wanted to follow us up and over the garden gate, so I tossed him a ladder. Not my fault if he doesn't know how to properly climb one." I paused and looked about the room. I could see Stanley sitting there, amiably, but no little brother. "So, he injured himself, did he? Out for a long time I suspect?"

"You needn't worry about his health, he's fine. I just didn't want him finding you quite yet...I still need your services regarding Robert Jones. No, my brother is having a little chat with Al at the moment."

"I don't see how, since we had him bound and gagged before we stole those ladders. Come to think of it, I mentioned something about having stolen the ladders to your brother. Maybe he went over to make sure Al—"

"That's not important," Cambria announced. "What's important is what's in this box. I suspect it has something to do with Tasia Everett."

"Well, whatever you think," countered Sonia, "you need to hand it over to me now, it's my property."

"I don't think so, Dr. Abbot," Cambria said. "Stanley, hand me a screwdriver."

Stanley found one in the drawer beside the sink and tossed it across the table. Cambria snatched it up and went to work. Once one side was off, she pulled out a black urn.

"Ha!" she exclaimed. "I wonder who lives in here?"

"I don't think it's Jeannie," I said.

"Give that to me!" demanded Sonia.

"No! This is evidence. Look, Professor Telsmith, it's got the name written on it right here," said Cambria pointing at the lettering with her finger. "I don't have my glasses. Could you read it out to us all?"

I took the urn and made out the word letter by letter: "S-P-O-T."

Sonia eyed both of us. She didn't know whether to scream with anger or laugh in mockery, so she said coolly, "Do you really think that if I killed Tasia Everett I would keep her ashes? I would just spread them along a country road and toss the urn in the river. And how would I get her cremated? 'Don't look now Mr. Cremator, but I'm going to slip a body into your oven while you're not looking. Tell me when the timer goes off.'"

She had a point.

"But you mentioned a crematorium," Cambria said.

"Whatever are you talking about?" responded Sonia.

"On Midterm Party Night, about midnight. On your porch."

Sonia raised her chin and eyebrows and looked sideways at Cambria, a bit like a billy goat ready to land a smacker on someone's forehead. "Have you been spying on me?"

"You did mention a crematorium at that time, didn't you?" I interjected.

"Very probably. My brother had phoned me earlier that day to say he was up in Omaha but would be down in Aspinwall for the night because of all the parties going on. I told him he could sleep at my place and asked him to pick up Spot at Gentle Rest Pet Crematorium, because I'd never had the chance to do so myself. When he showed up at the door, the first thing I asked him was if he'd made it to the crematorium."

"And Spot found himself a place under your

birdbath," I said solemnly as I ceremoniously handed the urn over to her.

She took it in hand and looked upon it tenderly. "I thought it a fitting memorial. He so loved to chase after birds from bush to bush."

She then took a deep breath and said, "All of you, Stanley included since you told him of your plans for tonight, are in trouble with the law. Any teaching position or scholarship you might have is now in jeopardy. I trust, then, if I am not to press charges, you will all keep mum about Robert Jones."

Sonia set the urn aside, put her elbows on the table and folded her hands. "Take a seat," she told us.

After we sat down, she resumed, "What I am about to tell you is very confidential, but I need help in my investigation as a member of the college's ethics committee. Here," she said as she lifted her satchel onto the table, opened it, and handed us forms. "Please sign these documents which will bind you to confidentiality."

I half smiled to myself. I doubted the forms were anything official or binding, but I went along with her charade.

Once we'd signed and she had collected them, she continued by saying, "I've managed to find out something about this Robert Jones, who is connected in some way with Henry Langstrom, and I'm afraid the connection may involve something unethical, something that would do harm to the reputation of our school. But I don't want to make any false accusations, mind you, so I need to find out the details for myself first, before bringing the evidence to the attention of President Larimer.

"I should add that I found out a bit more about Robert Jones from a colleague from another university. He said his wife knew Henry back in the day, when Henry was a TA. She had heard, from one of Henry's students, that Henry had an altercation of some sort with a student named Robert Jones. The argument got heated out in the parking lot near the cafeteria, and the friend remembers Jones struggling to find words but finally saying, 'Have you no sense of decency, Mr. Langstrom!' She said it reminded her of the McCarthy hearings back in the 1950s, when a lawyer asked Senator McCarthy the same thing. This Jones was, apparently, a shy individual, not handsome, but clever and always well dressed and manicured. I don't know if that helps us, but psychologically it may indicate something."

"You're not suggesting some sort of

stereotype, are you?" Cambria asked. "That all gay men are shy and clever but not attractive to women? Because it's not true."

I must say this declaration from Cambria surprised me.

"No, but it's not contradictory," Sonia claimed, "and it may just explain Henry's troubles with his wife, but that's not important. What is important is that Henry may have exploited the poor student, taken advantage of him in some way. I hope it's not true, but since I'm on the ethics committee, I must look into it."

"Well," I said, "all we need to do is contact this Robert Jones and find out."

"Unfortunately," said Sonia, "'Robert Jones' is a very common name and I haven't been able to locate him. But I'm sure we will in time, but it's not a given that Robert Jones, if he was involved in something reprehensible, will tell us anything. That's why you need to find out what type of correspondence is going on between Henry and Jones."

Sonia offered to give Cambria a lift back to the dorm, an offer that couldn't rationally be declined.

After they left, I sat down with Stanley and recounted the evening's events. The only thing he retained out of the whole affair was that I spent an interesting evening with Cambria. He suggested I ask her out on a date, so I had to explain that the armistice between us seemed to only work as long as we were searching for Tasia.

15

The next day, Tuesday, ran its course without incident until near five o'clock when I stopped by the Bookshire for an iced caramel coffee. I don't know how long Cambria had been waiting for me to drop by, but she was past the midpoint of her book. She signaled me as soon as she realized I was about to leave the shop with my drink.

"I see you are one of the people of the book," I joked as I took a seat opposite her.

"You know," she answered with her sanctimonious voice, "that's something your type will never understand!"

The words "What do you mean?" came out of my mouth before I could suppress them. I should have known from her prophetic tenor that I was walking into a trap.

"I mean that you say, 'Oh, Judaism is a religion of the book,' or, 'Christianity is a religion of the book.' More nonsensicality. Did Peter row about in his boat and say, 'I'm a disciple of a book'?"

"I didn't know he used a boat, I thought, perhaps, he had learned to walk on water."

"Christianity is not a religion of the book; it is a religion of the Spirit. Only someone who has never experienced God's Spirit can say, 'It's a religion of the book!'"

"It's just a way of saying that for Christians like you, the Bible defines the one and only true religion. It's infallible, has no mistakes. Which is ludicrous when you see Mark, Matthew, and Luke tell different versions of what was originally the same story. Did angels appear in the sky at Christ's birth? Luke says yes, Matthew doesn't mention any. One of them has to be wrong."

"You know, when I was in high school, I couldn't get to school one morning because there was a snowbank waist-high blocking my road, which is Road 732."

"What a relief for your teachers."

"No, because the snowplow came along and cleared the road and I made it to the second period."

"At least one teacher was happy."

"The next day, when I got to that first class,

the one I'd missed the day before, I told the teacher about the waist-high snowbank. Then my neighbor, Gallagher, came in, and he told the teacher that he was stopped by a three-foot high snowbank at Road 732. A little while later, Alice came in and said there was a six-foot snowbank blocking Road 732."

"It wasn't Alice Pitchner was it? She would have pulled the snowbank down."

"Nope, don't know who Alice Pitchner is."

"Your Alice isn't a friend of yours, is she?"

"Not particularly."

"Well, then, I will call her a liar."

"And you would be wrong. Mr. Rotlib put himself in front of the class and said we just had an excellent example of how different versions of a single story got into the Bible. Different versions, but all true. 'Waist high and three feet,' he said, 'are synonyms. It's just two different people expressing the same idea with different words.'"

"And Alice's 'six feet' was hyperbole?"

"No, Alice lived down the road on the other side of the snowbank, so on her side it was six feet. On my side it was three feet, or waist-high if you prefer. We all three were right. And that's not taking into account if we were to translate all three versions into French, and then translate my version into French by fifty different translators. We'd get even more synonyms and yet all renditions would be correct. Same goes for Matthew, Mark, and Luke! God doesn't lose sight of the forest for the tree like you skeptics."

"There's more involved than synonyms in the differences between the different gospels."

"For instance?"

"Number one, Jesus' sermon. It's different in Matthew than it is in Luke. In Matthew, Jesus is on a mountain, in Luke he's on a plain. In Matthew Jesus begins by opening his mouth, in Luke by looking up in the sky. Matthew gives eight beatitudes and Luke only four, Matthew says the poor in spirit are blessed, Luke says poor people are blessed, in Luke Jesus says woe to those who are rich, full of food, laughing, and spoken well of, because they're going to pay for it, but Matthew doesn't give a 'woe' about anybody. There, does that settle it?"

"Only for someone with blinders. Look about you. Have you ever heard of a politician? Have you ever heard a politician speak?"

"What do Matthew and Luke have to do with a politician? Are you admitting they're liars?"

"No, I'm talking about their speaking method, not their moral character. Think about it, a politician gives a stump speech, always hitting on the main problems he's concerned about and what his solutions are. The speech varies in length according to the time he has to deliver it, and it varies a bit in content and perspective depending upon his audience and current events. But it is essentially the same speech he gives everywhere."

"You mean like a stump speech?"

"Exactly, but it's not just something politicians do. You guys do it too! Think of Professor Langstrom. I'm sure he gives the same lecture on Constantine every semester. It no doubt varies in length and content a bit from one lecture to the next, depending on how far ahead or behind he is in his lecture schedule. But I also bet, if you go ask an alumnus of fifteen years ago to show us his lecture notes, his notes will correspond pretty well with lecture notes jotted down by a student taking Langstrom's class today. Jesus no doubt preached his stump sermon at least once a week, probably over fifty times a year."

"That must have been monotonous for his disciples."

She ignored what I esteemed to be a very good observation by blustering on and asking, "What's the probability that Matthew and Luke reported on the very same sermon he gave on the first Sabbath in the third month of the second year of his ministry? Zero. What's the probability they combined several versions of his sermon? Pretty good. What's the probability that they'll have similar themes in their accounts of Jesus' stump speech and several differences? One-hundred percent! The thing to keep in mind is that they both wanted to report on Jesus' stump speech and they essentially gave us the same central message that Jesus presented."

"I thought we had an agreement, an armistice," I finally said.

"We do. You don't bring up the Bible and I don't talk Bible."

"And yet here you babble on."

"You're the one who said I was 'one of the people of the Book,' and the Book is the Bible."

"Okay," I said taking a sip of my iced caramel coffee with one hand and acting like I was sprinkling her head with holy water with the other, "I absolve you of being one of the people of the book. What is it you want to see me about?"

"I think we need to talk to Jennifer."

"Jennifer?"

"Tasia's roommate."

"Any good reason?"

"Yes, I have it from an excellent source, Angela, that Jennifer and Tasia argued on the morning of Tasia's disappearance."

"About what?"

"That's what we need to find out."

***

About supper time, Cambria and I made our way over to Toine Barada Gym to see if we could find Jennifer. The girl is fairly easy to spot, she's six-foot four and lanky. She was recruited for the River Rats women's volleyball team for a single purpose: To tower over an opponent at the net and drill her face with a volleyball.

We waited patiently at the gym's exit, knowing tonight's practice was ending. The gym was an odd building. As I've intimated elsewhere, it was obvious that the college had contracted a morning group of rural coffee drinkers, a majority being farmers, to design the building. Its tin roof and siding could easily house a score of the most up-to-date combines.

Within ten or fifteen minutes the exit door sprung open and the female athletes began to issue forth, mostly in little groups of two or three. When Jennifer exited, Cambria immediately called out to her to separate her from her friends. The tactic worked as I saw Jennifer say something to her little coterie before coming to us, probably something like, "Oh, God, not her! I'll see you later."

"What is it?" she asked, looking down upon us.

I had a hard time imagining how I was going to interrogate this young lady. Normally, as a detective, you expect to have your suspect seated below you and sweating under the sheriff's searchlight. But even seated, I think Jennifer would still have been looking down on me.

Her height had absolutely no effect on Cambria. "We need to ask you a few questions about Tasia."

Jennifer didn't look at Cambria. Rather she held a steady side glance aimed at me. I supposed that since I was a professor, I would be the one explaining. I took the cue. "We're just trying to find out what happened to your roommate, we're concerned. We know she's sent you some postcards, but all the same, it just seems very peculiar. We hope nothing has happened to her."

"I agree," said Jennifer. "Not at all like her to send a postcard. Way too literary. But let's go into the park and have a seat to discuss this more eye to eye. It's irritating looking down on people's hairlines all the time."

I didn't say anything, but I could have pointed out that looking up at someone's nasal hairs was no more pleasant.

Governor Morehead City Park, popularly known as Governor's Park, was just around the bend of the main drag through campus. North of the bend, the street was known as Girard Street, south of the bend it was appropriately called Park Avenue, and it leads on down to the Bookshire. The park itself is mostly at a forty-five-degree slope, but there's a flat area at the bottom with swing set, an outdoor grill, and a picnic table.

Sitting down at the table across from Jennifer, I found her to be in the right and I in the wrong. She must be three-fourths legs.

"The postcards," Jennifer said, "are so out of sync with Tasia. Especially her just leaving all her clothes and things. She was very attached to her wardrobe."

Cambria, being true to herself, came directly to the point. "We understand you had an argument with her the morning of her disappearance."

Jennifer didn't seem bothered by the

accusation. "We certainly did! Or, rather, I told her off. She didn't say much. I was angry with her for going through my things. I opened my dresser drawer and found my blouse folded in a way I don't fold it. So, I called her out on it."

"What did she say?" I asked.

"She said she was just borrowing some of my sweatpants and a top because she didn't have any. I told her they wouldn't fit, and she said all she had to do was roll up the sleeves and pant legs."

"Can't run very far like that," I observed.

"No, it was crazy, but Tasia is like that."

"Did you let her have them?"

"I never checked to see if she really took any. To be honest, I have several pair, and though I would recognize if something's folded the wrong way, I don't know if I'd actually realize if a pair was missing. It's just that I knew she'd been snooping around in my things and I didn't like it. So, I told her to stay out of my dresser in the future or I'd go get a volleyball and rearrange her face with it."

***

When we had finished interviewing Jennifer, Cambria accompanied me back to my car, but before she let me escape, she insisted we review all the information we had thus far, and justified the idea by saying Poirot often did this with Hastings. She didn't clarify which one of us was which.

"Well," I said, "you're right, it's very much like a Poirot mystery, except there is one difference."

"How so?" she asked.

"Just list the information we have, and I'll tell you."

"I think you can give us a summary, Hastings."

"Okay," I conceded, "I believe we have several disconnected facts; to wit: Tasia went to Boston, Jennifer had an argument with Tasia, Tasia made it to Barton's party, Barton showed some indiscrete interest in Tasia, Franky was miffed, Franky saw Tasia walking up from the Bookshire toward the dorm around eleven-thirty Friday night, and Tasia allegedly has written postcards to Jennifer saying she has resigned her college career."

"That's a very good list," she said. I believed she was about to adopt a Belgian accent and add a "*n'est-ce pas?*" but instead she asked, "So, what's the difference with a Poirot mystery?"

"We don't have Poirot to link all the facts

together."

This bothered Cambria, and she stopped walking so she could hold her chin up and search the skies for a revelation from on high, perhaps as the apostles had done in that room in Jerusalem. Then her eyes brightened up as if she'd been hit by a tongue of fire. "Maybe we're looking at all this too narrowly."

It was my turn to say, "How so?"

"Let's figure in the faculty as well and see what friction there is between them, and then we'll factor in Tasia."

"Well, I see you are the one with the little grey cells," I said.

"All right, then, Hastings, tell me anything you haven't told me so far about trouble between faculty members."

I related to her the whole incident with Sonia, when Langstrom and Al wanted me to hack into her computer. She liked best the part about me being caught in Sonia's bedroom, but what surprised her most was, of course, Sonia's directive that I get into Langstrom's computer to find out about Robert Jones, especially if she were on the ethics committee.

Then Cambria posed an apparently random question: "I wonder if there's a link between this Robert Jones and Tasia? What did you find on

Dr. Langstrom's computer?"

"Nothing," I said sheepishly, "I don't know his password."

I felt very little like James Bond at this point and more and more like Inspector Clouseau. "I did see his phone on his desk, and I took a look at his calls received." I didn't think my phone snooping relevant, but I wanted to convince her, and perhaps myself, that I had at least accomplished something spy-worthy.

"As far as I could tell," I added, "there were no calls from a Robert Jones. Of course, any one of the incoming calls that just listed a number might have been Robert Jones. I would have no way of knowing, and neither would James Bond."

"James Bond?" she giggled. "You think you're like James Bond?"

"Given an English accent, yes. I was as resourceful, I thought of looking at Langstrom's phone contacts. No Robert Jones there either, by the way...although he did have one mysterious contact listed simply as 'MM'. All I could think of was Marilyn Monroe, but then that's a problem a lot of twentieth century movie buffs have." I dug out my wallet, opened it, then showed her the index card with the number.

"Call it," Cambria ordered.

I brought out my phone and punched in the numbers.

"Well," said Cambria as it rang, "are you going to put it on speaker?"

I put it on speaker. A woman answered. I couldn't tell the age. And before I responded, I could hear Cambria whispering, "Ask her about Robert Jones."

"Hello, ugh, Hello ma'am. I'm calling from Aspinwall College, and I was wondering if you knew Robert Jones."

"Robert? Why? Who is this?"

"W-well, this is...this is Professor Langstrom."

"No it isn't!" She went on to call me a name or two, both of which were incorrect, but the gist of our little chat was that I had better butt out of things I knew nothing about. She ended the tête-à-tête by saying she had my number and was going to track me down. I was about to respond that I was going to return the favor, but she must have had an errand to run because she hung up before I could.

16

As I opened the door to my Batteredmobile to leave, I told Cambria that in spite of the fact that we'd learned very little of significance, it had been an interesting evening. As usual, she disagreed.

"On the contrary, I found it telling that when you asked MM about Robert Jones, she said, 'Robert? Why?' She didn't say 'Robert who?' We now know two people who know Robert Jones personally. First, Dr. Langstrom, who, back in his TA days, had an altercation with Robert Jones, who was probably a student of his, given that they knew each other well enough to have an argument. And second, this woman, MM."

"Al knows about him. And Sonia seems to know something too," I added.

"We won't count Dr. Abbot because she knows no more than we do."

I leaned on the top of the car door. "Though

I don't see how knowing anything about Robert Jones can lead us to finding out what happened to Tasia."

"I've got a hunch."

"Feminine intuition?" I asked mockingly.

"You obviously don't understand the whole nature and purpose of feminine intuition. God gave it to us women so we could help you guys out when your brains fail you. So women are using it all the time."

"I suppose Eve had a hunch that the apple was good?"

"Well, we can't get them all right, but Rahab's hunch that she should help Joshua panned out. Besides," she added, "it reminds me of Florence Flynn."

"Go on."

"One day, when I was in tenth grade, my friend Kelly Napier saw Florence Flynn, normally a good and well-behaved student, put a domesticated rat in Mrs. Sheffield's desk drawer. Mrs. Sheffield was our English teacher and she could scream extremely well, and proved it. Later in the day, when I came back from the shower after a round of basketball, which the PE teacher made me participate in, I discovered my bra was missing from my locker, which I had left open. So, I went to Barb

Sitwith's locker, took her purse out of it, extracted a twenty-dollar bill, and told her I was going to use the money to buy myself a new bra."

"Seems perfectly logical," I said sarcastically. "What happened next?"

"She told me where my bra was, and once I'd retrieved it, I gave her back the twenty dollars."

"So where was it?"

"Hanging on the doorknob to the principal's office."

"Not to sound critical or anything, but I don't quite see the link between the rat and the bra."

"There is one, but you have to be a woman to understand it."

"Try me."

"Florence and Barb were best friends."

"So," I tried, "if one of the two was acting up, pulling a prank, then the other might be pulling a prank as well. Is that it?"

"I'll make a woman out of you yet."

"No, I still think it's far-fetched."

She looked at me with pity, then said, "I suppose I should also tell you that the fact that MM doesn't want you interfering also tells us something significant."

"Yeah, and my male intuition tells me it's a

something we don't know anything about."

"Something you don't know anything about," she said. "I'll see you in class tomorrow. The lecture's on Charlemagne isn't it? The Church Council of 799, no doubt?"

When she mentioned the Church, a popular adage popped into my mind: "First twenty times shame on me," or something to that effect. I kept my silence.

"You know," she insisted, "when the heresy of adoptionism was rejected."

"I won't fall for it this time," I warned her.

I could have sworn that she, before leaving, vacillated between giving me a hug and just telling me a plain good-bye. Finally, she said, after hesitating, "Have a good evening, Professor Telsmith." I hoped I had been imagining things.

***

This thought of Cambria warming up to me again muddled my head until I turned northbound onto Highway 67. As soon as one comes onto the highway there is an S-curve that grabs one's attention. On the right side is an oft flooded field that serves as a landing strip, depending upon the season, for ducks, geese, seagulls, and pelicans. It always struck me as odd that seagulls and pelicans find a home in Nebraska, but then again Henry, Al, and Sim landed here as well. And Tasia, she was an odd bird.

As I crossed the bridge leading into the village of Nemaha, I thought about the investigation. It seemed that if harm indeed had come to our odd bird that we had two groups of suspects: student suspects and faculty suspects.

I ran through my mind all the students and what their attitudes were regarding Tasia. Barton and Franky seemed to appreciate her, Angela and Jennifer, and even Cambria, didn't. Hmmm, I thought, there seems to be a male, female divide.

But other than attitude, was there any reason to make Tasia disappear?

I recalled Al saying, "I don't see how Barton would want any harm done to Tasia." But I now asked myself, "Do we really know Barton well enough to make that assessment?" Maybe he was really obsessed with her. "She's hot!" he had said, and with conviction. And she was with him the night of the party. What if he had taken her into his house and made advances and she resisted? Perhaps he killed her and hid her in a closet until he had an opportunity to get rid of the body. Any body dropped into the Missouri, especially if weighted down, would disappear under yards of sediment within no time.

I decided to question Barton the next day, after class.

***

When I arrived home, I saw an unknown automobile parked in my driveway. Upon entering the house, I found the car owner sitting at our kitchen table. It was Angela.

Standing before the sink was Stanley, washing up dishes. Apparently the two had just finished supper. A romantic one I gauged, given the presence of burning candles.

"I've just told Angela all about our victory at state, my senior year," said Stanley as he set a plate in the dishrack.

Angela turned to me and her somewhat weak smile blossomed. "Tristan, I mean...well, do you really mind if I call you Tristan when we're not in class?"

"You can call me whatever you want," I said. This was true. I really don't mind students calling me by my first name as long as they remained respectful.

Her smile was now in full bloom. "Really?

Well, come sit with us. What have you been up to?"

I obliged her and sat down. "I'm trying to find out what happened to Tasia."

Her smile wilted a bit. "Her?" she asked. She looked down meditatively at the cup of tea placed in front of her. "Yes," she said, "I think it's strange, her disappearance. I worry about her. I hope she found someone who truly loves her, and that she ran off with him. Don't you, Tristan?"

"Oh, yes, that would be better than if harm had befallen her."

"And," added Angela, "she really wasn't interested in studies, so she won't be missed as a student, I don't think."

"Well," I said hesitantly, "I don't know if I would say she wouldn't be missed. I try to appreciate all of our students."

"You know what I'm getting at, though, don't you? She's not really someone you could identify with, was she?"

"Perhaps not academically."

"Not academically?" she said somewhat mechanically. "Well, then, I suppose it's just as well she's gone. After all, we are at college. There's no reason to be here, if you're not interested in studies."

"Yes," said Stanley, supporting Angela's line of reasoning. "It's really good riddance, then, isn't it?"

Angela glanced approvingly at Stanley and rose from the table. It's really been nice of you to keep me, Stanley, and even make dinner. It was wonderful, but I definitely must get back and study. But Tristan, since Stanley's doing the dishes, could you walk me to my car?"

I agreed and opened the front door for her. Once outside she looked out over Brownville and said, "It's so beautiful here, romantic even, with fall."

Indeed, with the fading green, the dark red, and the bright yellow and orange tones of autumn coloring our trees and shrubs, it was beautifully romantic.

"I can see why you chose this house," she continued, "with its second story window looking out over this paradise. I would love it here too. It's an inspiration to read, think, and write. All you need is a little music filling the air."

I didn't really have anything more to add, so I remained silent.

Finally, she said, still looking off into the distance, "Tasia would not have appreciated this."

"You're probably right," I admitted.

"Tristan," she said, turning to me. "Perhaps I can come again. And you really shouldn't bother yourself with Tasia. I'm sure she wouldn't have given you a second thought had you disappeared. That's just the way she was."

"Well," I responded, "Stanley and I would be glad to have you over again, sometime. So, thanks for dropping by, and I'll see you in class."

We exchanged a word or two more, but she eventually got into her car and headed down to Aspinwall. When I went back inside, I found Stanley in a merry mood and pouring out two whiskeys. We drank to Angela's health, and I told him she wished to come back soon, and he found that reason enough to have a second round.

***

During Wednesday's class I steered clear of adoptionism and explained how Charlemagne had built up an empire without money, or at least with very little of it compared to the Romans and many other imperially-minded people. Alexander, you've no doubt heard, ultimately financed his ephemeral empire with the gettings from Persepolis. Charlemagne's system, what historians have dubbed "feudal," would be, if known to them, the envy of every Republican voter: a fixed tax.

If you produced three bushels of wheat annually—one for the IRS, one for your stomach, and one for sowing next year's crop—then all you had to do to make a substantial profit was devise a way to grow four bushels. Hence the moldboard plow: to overturn previously untillable soil; the horseshoe: to give grip to the horse pulling it; and the shoulder harness: to allow the horse to breathe while dragging about your new moldboard. And why a horse? Because the equine could walk at a faster rate than the traditional bovine. End result? One more bushel. Profit.

As I came to this point in my lecture, my eyes fell upon Tasia's empty seat. Or at least the one she had left next to Franky. And something clicked in my brain: The word "profit." That's something we haven't considered. Was there money linked to Tasia?

I continued on in the lecture and commented upon how Christianity had transformed civilization in the West and would ultimately transform things in the world. These were things not underscored by the textbook, and for a reason. When shaping young minds, textbook authors don't want to confuse their readership by presenting more than one point of view. I, however, believe a good historian presents all sides, because truth will ultimately win the day. I think that's as close to faith as I get, but it serves me well.

"The Christian religion," I said at one point, "spawned a progressive spirit in western civilization, which, for better or worse, would one day enable the Europeans to overspread the world and dominate it."

I wasn't saying other religions were no good while Christianity was. I would put them all in the same box and drop them off at Goodwill if I had my way. But it is hard to deny, even for a Miscreant, that Christianity, unlike all other religions and cultures, which were backward looking and hoping to recreate some sort of ancestral golden era, was decidedly forward looking.

This progressive spirit, of course, didn't apply to my hermits, but it did apply to nearly everyone else. By and large, Christians ultimately could have cared less as to how things were done, whether by an ox, like grandpa had done, or by a horse, like nobody had done before.

In a word, Christianity was primarily

concerned about "ethics." It was the why, not the how that counted.

I wasn't claiming that medieval Christians didn't follow traditions, they did, but it wasn't crucial, no pun intended, to their belief system. In sum, Christianity freed humanity from technologies rooted in tradition. As a result, Europeans were soon firing off canons, setting sail in late model caravels, and conquering empires. All in the name of God, of course.

"But we mustn't just focus on the canons," I pointed out. "The Christians did not just bring us death and destruction, they also, rather ironically, highlighted ethics as our primary concern as human beings: the ideas of guilt, repentance, and reconciliation became part and parcel of the western conscience.

"That's why no other culture," I emphasized, "does the things that western countries, like the United States, do. And even though we're no longer Christian, we've retained this focus on guilt, repentance, and reconciliation.

"What other country would even consider condemning itself for a wrong, and then propose reparations? Think about it. The Puritans hung the witches, but then they repented of it and provided compensation for the families who had lost loved ones in the witch hunt. Americans regret the harm done to Native Americans, the enslavement of Africans, the treatment of African Americans as second-class citizens under Jim Crow, the internment of Japanese Americans during World War II. Not only do they regret it, but they ask for forgiveness and try to amend by rebuilding tribes, creating the Freedmen's Bureau, passing affirmative action legislation, paying reparations to the Japanese interned during World War II. Does China or Iran feel guilty about policies of the past or present? Do they ask forgiveness of the Uyghurs or the Yazidi? Do the Arabs ask forgiveness for their conquest of Palestine, or the way they treated Jews and Christians as second-class citizens? No, and they really can't be blamed. It's not part of their national conscience. Not part of their cultural inheritance."

Anyway, the lecture was adequate to put half the class to sleep. My record is three-fourths, but that was after some unwitting student asked me to tell them about my dissertation on hermits.

Nonetheless, as I heard myself detail the contributions that Christianity made to the development of western civilization, I noticed Cambria visibly shaken and nodding in agreement. Then it donned on me, in seeing her face teary-eyed, why she was so passionate about finding out what happened to Tasia: She felt guilty somehow.

17

When class was over, I managed to buttonhole Barton, as they say in those twentieth-century novels. It wasn't hard to find a reason, Barton never turns in an assignment on time, so I got his attention by asking about his essay comparing Seneca's *Phaedra* with the Apostle Paul's epistle to the Romans. The assignment is an excellent exercise in comparing two worldviews. According to Seneca, it's up to an individual's willpower to pursue a virtuous and fulfilling life. According to Paul, humans are incapable of doing this on their own. I doubt Barton had any ambition to follow either Seneca or Paul. He was more of the Epicurean stripe.

"Oh, yeah," he said with a ready explanation. "I had it saved on my laptop, but it got fried during that storm."

"But that was a nice party you had."

"Thanks, man. I know how to have a good time."

Yes, definitely an Epicurean.

Since I really wasn't interested in reading his essay at the moment, I didn't bring up the apparently little-known fact that we had not had a storm during the week he was to write it, and said instead, "You can hand it in Friday, but there will be ten-percent taken off your grade."

As I was saying this, I saw, behind Barton, a shadow against the doorframe. Someone lingered nearby.

"Thanks, man," Barton said.

"Also," I said, before he rushed off to indulge in his next pleasure, "I wanted to ask you about Tasia."

"Sure, seems everyone's asking me about her," he said somewhat bitterly. "She's a phony if you ask me."

"Well, she is a tease, that's true, but when's the last time you saw her?"

The shadow now metamorphosed into Cambria as she, all ears, stepped forward and stood behind Barton.

"At the party," Barton said.

"She didn't stay over, or you didn't go with her somewhere?" I asked.

"Nope, but," he said with a sly smile, "I did

tell her I knew how to get money to buy those One Direction tickets for the pit, and that caught her attention."

"And what did she say to that?"

"She asked me how I was going to get the money. I told her it was easy, you just pop open the change machine at Langdon Bridge Car Wash. It's full of money. I was just jokin' around though, 'cause that's the way I am."

"So, did she say she'd go with you to see One Direction?" I wanted to know if she had plans for the future, other than dropping out of college.

"No," he said, "but I think she'd like to go, but she was playing hard to get. She said she was after bigger game." Then he chuckled and added, "So I asked her if people did a lot of hunting where she came from. You know, like a joke."

I thought that was all he had to say, but he stood there, almost immobile, looking up at the ceiling. Obviously thinking back to the night, retrieving a memory. Before long he said, "You know, now that I think about it, she got talking kind of weird like after that."

"How so?"

"She said, 'You'll never know where I come from,' so I said, 'I suppose I could find out, I know your name.' Then she said, 'You don't know my name, you haven't a clue.' That turned me off. But it wasn't so much what she said, it's the way she said it. Spiteful like...that last part: 'You haven't a clue.' I mean jokin' around's great, but she was acting like she was superior to everybody else. Like I wasn't in her class."

"That must have upset you."

"Yeah."

"And she left, and you didn't see her again?"

He didn't answer immediately. Maybe he was trying to remember. Then he said, "And I don't plan on ever seeing her again, even if I get the money for One Direction. Hell, I'd rather ask Cambria to go with me than her."

"Well, that might not be difficult to do."

Cambria then made her presence known. "Not interested, Barton, but not because you're too stupid or because you're too smart. One Direction just isn't my thing."

Barton turned, obviously ill at ease. "Hey, man, Cambria. Ummm—"

Cambria ignored his embarrassment and asked, "What did you mean when you said, 'everyone's asking me about her'?"

It took a second or two for Barton to regather his thoughts, but finally he said, "The police."

"The Aspinwall police?" I asked.

"Not exactly," said Cambria. "It would be the sheriff. Aspinwall isn't big enough to support a separate police department."

"You mean Sheriff Abbot?"

"He wasn't there," said Barton. "I suppose it was a couple of his deputies. They said they're looking into 'the Tasia Everett case' and wanted to know if I knew her real name.

"I said 'Tasia Everett?' and they told me to quit covering for her. Then they said they knew that I was close to her, because someone said I was, so I'd better tell them what her real name is. I told 'em it was news to me if Tasia Everett wasn't her name. That's why I said she was a phony.

"They finally believed me; I think. Anyway, they left and didn't say they would be comin' back."

This bit of information threw me, and I could only manage a "What in the world?" and a "Well I'll be!" response.

"Yeah, dude, weird like. I tell you; I'm not missing her."

I was so muddled to learn that "Tasia Everett" was an alias that my brain just went on autopilot. Fortunately, it had been programmed by enough episodes of *Midsomer Murders* to spontaneously ask, "And what time did Tasia leave your party?"

"She was gone by...." He looked up at the ceiling again, apparently that's where he got all his ideas from. "Let's see, I went into the house around eleven and I laid down awhile. She had gone into the house to use the restroom, but that's the last I saw of her."

"While your party was going on, you took a nap?" I asked.

"Yeah, not for long. Maybe a half hour. You know, to recharge."

Cambria turned to me and asked, "And she wasn't there when you got back, was she, Professor Telsmith?"

"I can't really say," I replied. "I didn't spend much time at the party after that, wasn't looking for her."

"Hmmm," Cambria said, perplexed.

"Well," said Barton, "if I napped for a half hour, then it was more likely she was gone by eleven thirty, because when I came out there was still a half-hour left before midnight and I did take a walk around the party saying 'Hi' to everybody, and I didn't come across Tasia. Trust me, I would have remembered. In fact, Jennifer asked me if I'd seen her a little bit afterwards, maybe around 11:35. She said she tried to call her, but her phone was off."

"What did Jennifer want her for?"

"I think she was going to ask her if she wanted a lift back to the dorm, since she was leaving the party."

"Okay," I said. "By eleven thirty or eleven thirty-five p.m. she was gone."

"Yep," said Barton. "Anything else?"

"No, just remember to get your paper in on Friday."

"Sure thing, Teach." And with that, he left.

"Tasia Everett is not Tasia Everett," I said more to myself than to Cambria as she stepped toward me. "So, maybe she didn't need to bother about dropping a class after all. But why come to college under an assumed name? Why suddenly leave?"

Leaning up against the computer workstation table, I asked Cambria, "Is she under the witness protection program?"

"Or maybe," Cambria offered, "someone has figured out she wasn't who she said she was, so she took off. But then why send a postcard? And why say to Barton, 'You don't know my name'?"

I thought about this for a bit, humming and hawing, then I came up with a theory. "'Tasia' is short for 'Anastasia,' and Anastasia can mean a couple of things, the first one being 'resurrection.'"

"She may be a vamp," said Cambria, "but only figuratively. She's certainly not Jesus Christ."

"Don't use that to bring in your religious indoctrination."

"You're the one talking resurrection."

"Nope, not going to fall for it. But let's see if you fall for this: I know what the second thing is that Anastasia might stand for. It's my secret."

"No, that's not part of the deal. No secrets from me if we're going to investigate together: So, what's the second thing?"

"Anastasia Romanov was the Czar's daughter who supposedly escaped execution. A woman claiming to be her showed up in the U.S., but she was an imposter who, I suppose, hoped to get her hands on the Romanov jewels. Her real name was Franziska something."

"So Tasia is like Franziska Something claiming to be Anastasia Romanov."

"I think so, but only insofar as she had an alias. Kind of like a game. She heard of this woman taking on a fake name, Anastasia, and thought it would be slick to use the name herself. She can't be claiming to be Anastasia Romanov, she'd have to be over a hundred years old."

We both stood there pondering. Eventually Cambria asked out loud the question we both were pondering, "But how does any of this fit in with all the rest we've found out?"

A lightning bolt hit me. "The stump speech!" I exclaimed.

Cambria gave me one of those looks an owl might give when hit by a stalag search light.

"Yes," I insisted. "I'm thinking of your stump speech theory about Jesus."

"Theory? Why is it fact when you skeptics make up something about Jesus but when somebody who actually knows Jesus and talks with him every day comes up with something it's just a theory?"

"Okay, your stump speech observation."

"That's better, but I still don't follow."

"Well, to be honest, you shouldn't, because it's a very tenuous connection, but it gave me an idea. Both Matthew and Luke were using Jesus' stump speech to get his message across, i.e. to love one another. Both Tasia and I were using gum to get into Langstrom's office to get dirt on him."

"That's not even 'tenuous.' Not even in the same ballpark."

"Okay," I conceded, "but your stump speech idea somehow got me onto this idea. Imagine both Tasia and I were after the same sort of information: dirt on Langstrom. Now here's the gospel according to me: I go in, I try the computer, then I look at the phone and see the MM name and number. It really stands out. So, I call it. Now, Tasia has already been in Langstrom's office, at some point, and for the same purpose. Trying to get dirt on him. Why else would she go in there? Now, here's the gospel according to Tasia: She tries the computer, just like I did. Then she looks at his phone—"

"Oh my!" Cambria said, and not unlike Dorothy might have exclaimed in the *Wizard of Oz*.

"What is it?" I asked.

"Two things."

"Number one?"

"Your analogy is bonkers, but I think you've mastered feminine intuition."

"Number two?"

"Well, what you were about to say. She sees the MM number. It appears odd, strange, so she follows up on it. She finds out MM is in Boston. She goes there to talk with MM. She gets back to Aspinwall, but MM follows her and murders her. Who is MM?"

"Mary Murderess?" I ventured.

"We need to keep asking questions," Cambria said, "which means we need to question more people connected to Langstrom and Tasia, or whatever her name is. Is there anyone we've missed?"

"Well," I suggested, "we haven't considered Sim Garfield. He knew Tasia."

***

We decided to meet up with Sim in the afternoon, during his office hours, when he's required to be there but has nothing substantial to do. You would think a professor of political science would have a following of groupies, wiling away the hours with him mocking politicians, but Sim's gift for mockery extends to everyone so equitably that students avoid him.

When we reached the door, I knocked, and we immediately heard his voice telling us to come in.

Sim's office is on the second floor and has a window overlooking the campus. We found him standing in front of the glass observing the students and faculty below, crisscrossing each other along paths that radiated out of the center of the quad.

I gave him an upbeat "Hello!" so he would

know what type of sarcasm to employ. You don't want a scholar who's pleased with himself, like Sim is, saying something like "I suppose you've come to complain that your last grade was too high" if the target audience is not a student. In my case, I would expect him to say something like, "I suppose you've come to complain that the dean has assigned you too many classes to teach."

But rather than deliver a punch and then turn around to see his victim gasp, he just stood in place and asked, "You see that young scholar in the blue jacket and beige cargo pants walking towards us?"

We looked out the window and identified the student.

"He told me last night, via email, that he couldn't make it to the quiz this morning because his grandmother had passed away and he would be at her funeral today down in San Antonio. I believe that's in Texas." Sim said this with his hands clasped behind his back, as if admiring and critiquing a landscape by Van Gogh. "Must own a jet."

Cambria and I sat down in the two armchairs facing his desk.

"Tea?" he asked as he turned around. He stopped, suddenly realizing I had come with a student. "For two?" he added.

We took him up on the offer, which came with lemon cookies, and he sat down at his desk. As usual, he began the conversation. He asked me if I were prepared to present my hermits to The Social Sciences Club members on Friday evening at Stickers. I said they were very shy, but since I told them I would give them nothing to eat, they had agreed to come along.

After we finished our little chit chat about hermits, as people usually do when dipping lemon cookies in hot tea and sucking on them, I finally broached the matter at hand: Tasia Everett.

I told him we were worried about her, and I informed him about what Barton had said, how Tasia's name was an alias. Sim raised his eyebrows at this.

After a moment of silence, he uttered, "Really? I wonder if that's all that was fake about her?"

"I don't think so," I said softly, thinking of the background to her necklace.

"I couldn't tell you," said Cambria less softly. "But in our investigation, we're tracking down everyone's movements on the night she disappeared: Midterm Party Night."

"Oh, you're the Avengers," he responded with a hint of amusement. "Emma Peel and John Steed. Or is it Maxwell Smart and Agent 99?"

Cambria had no idea what he was talking about, but judging it superfluous, asked, "So, what were you doing that Friday night? And did you see Tasia?"

"Can't say I saw the girl," said Sim as he leaned back in his chair. If this had been the 1960s, he would have lit a cigar and blown a smoke ring into the air, and then shot a smaller one through the first one. Even without the accessory in hand, he nonetheless drew a deep breath before letting out, "That evening was rather quiet. Henry decided to call off our usual debauchery on Midterm Party Night. He wanted to get to bed early and sober. I had half a mind to go over there anyway." Sim went quiet for a moment, looking back toward the window, contemplating. Then he added, "Didn't do him a lick of good, because I didn't see him peddling 'round until 10 or maybe 10:30, when Julius took me for my morning walk."

I explained to Cambria that Julius was Sim's dog.

"If I'm understanding you correctly, Professor Garfield," Cambria pronounced with dragnet dryness, "on Friday night you did not go out or see anybody."

"I didn't say that. I said I didn't see Tasia, or whoever she is. I did also take Julius out late on Midterm Party Night."

"Is that something you usually do?"

Sim smiled at Cambria, but his eyes looked in my direction and he said, "I thought the Gestapo had gone out of fashion."

I felt a little tension in the air.

"He woke me up with his barking," he said more sharply, "so I thought he needed to go out and decorate somebody else's sidewalk." Sim paused. "You'd better be taking notes because I may quiz you on this later. I am a professor."

Cambria dug into her purse and produced a notepad and pen. "I remember most everything said to me, but you're right, I'll want to quote you verbatim."

"We took the usual route," he continued on at a walking pace to let Cambria keep up, "down Levee Road, up Holiday past Al's, then back west on Second and then up Lawrence to home again. Julius knows the path and he won't let me stray from it. I was right, by the way, and after he did his artwork, I saw a handful of students roaming about."

"Looking for the library?" I asked, hoping to

take some pressure out of the atmosphere.

Cambria blew the pressure right back into it with a stern "What were the names of the students?"

He said it was hard to identify every "suspect," as he put it. The night air, he recalled, had turned cool by then and people were buttoned up with hoods raised. He did give us the names of two of the four who said "Hi" to him. Neither one seemed to have anything to do with Tasia as far as we knew, but Cambria jotted down their names, nonetheless. The third one he couldn't recognize, a tubby Hispanic boy, maybe a high schooler.

Sim finished his testimony by saying he did catch a glimpse of the fourth one under a hood. "The streetlamp at Holiday and Second Streets illuminated his face from time to time. He was pacing back and forth, like he was trying to make up his mind about something."

"And?" I said encouragingly.

"I know him only by sight," he said, eyeing Cambria. "It was that nerdy looking fellow that hangs out with you...in the cafeteria."

"Franky?" she asked.

"Don't know his name."

She described Franky, as flatteringly as possible, sticking to the attributes of head and face: black hair, Brylcreemy; needle nose, a bit pimpled; glasses, big-framed and thickish; a weak chin underlaying a sometimes gaping mouth.

"Skinny but not tall? Skis for shoes?" added Sim.

We concluded it had to be our Franky. The fact that he crossed Sim's path didn't surprise us as we knew Franky was out and about Friday night and had reported seeing Tasia.

Then Cambria rebooted her detective instincts and asked Sim if he were sure that he saw Franky at Holiday and Second Streets.

"As sure as I am that a grandmother will die come finals week. The boy was very conspicuous by his nervous behavior. Like he couldn't make up his mind whether or not to cross the street toward the levee."

"And this was around eleven-thirty?" Cambria asked.

"Yes, now that I think about it, because it wasn't yet midnight when I went back to bed."

Cambria and I looked at each other wide-eyed.

"Is he your villain?" asked Sim.

Cambria shook her head sharply to say no. I had seen my four-year old nephew shake his head like that once, when I gave him a lick of tabasco sauce. "No, not Franky. He's okay."

Sim leaned forward again. I couldn't help but think of Vincent Price whispering a curse: "It's always the least suspected one in the movies. And in real life it's the quiet one, kind of a loner, skinny, wears glasses, a loser...that type."

Seeing Cambria's face whiten and suspecting she might soon be sick in Dr. Simeon Garfield's tea cup, I ended the interview and made excuses about needing to grade Barton's essay, which, I explained, "scrutinizes the disparities between Stoicism and Christianity as revealed through the writings of Seneca and the Apostle Paul." I escorted her out and offered to accompany her to her dorm, but she said she had other things to attend to. I suspected that whatever she had to do would involve her trying to clear Franky's name.

18

On Thursday morning, stepping out of the house into a bright morning, chilled with the autumn air, I felt rather perky and even high-spirited. The nascent sun breaking across the horizon seems to do that to me, except on weekends when sleeping is mandatory.

Climbing into the Batteredmobile and revving up the engine, I exited 215 South 6th Street, Brownville, Nebraska, at precisely eight a.m. A few minutes later, slaloming down and up the hills of Highway 67, I crossed by Cemetery Road on the left before descending into Nemaha village, which obliged me to press on the brakes and bring my speed down to a cool 40 miles-per-hour. Passing the market cafe, I saluted the farmers in the parking lot, who each flicked a friendly hand in the air in return, a Nebraskan courtesy.

Yes, the day held promise. Franky, one of those Bible-toters had been caught in a lie. I don't know why that made my heart sing, but it did, and it transferred to my lips readily. I could but think of John Lennon's song, "God." In it he wrapped religion all up nicely. The gist of it is to not believe in God, the Bible, or Jesus, because you only have to believe in yourself. I was singing the song as I pulled into Bookshire drive-thru.

"You just believe in yourself?" came a question over the speaker. "Must be pretty lonely. Do you believe in coffee?"

I told the speaker that I believed in hazelnut coffee with a shot of vanilla and caramel along with a blueberry scone.

Walking into Langstrom's office I found my chair and settled into it, finishing my scone.

"I agree," said Sim, looking at my coffee and then Langstrom's pot. "Better to order out, but this is cheaper."

"Oh," I said, looking at my Bookshire coffee, "I'm just celebrating, though I won't refuse a second cup from the communal pot afterwards."

"What's to celebrate? Did somebody steal that beater of yours?"

"No, no, although with the insurance money I might get me a car with a stationary hood. No,

I'm celebrating a student, Franky. He's one of the biblical clan and we caught him in flagrante delicto."

This caught Langstrom's attention. "Murder? Rape? Do tell me it was both, and vis a vis Sonia Abbot."

"No, but just as bad for their type: lying."

"About what?" asked Al.

"Sim might guess what I'm talking about. It's about this Franky seeing Tasia on the night of her disappearance. Either he didn't see her at all, or he didn't see her where he said he did. And the second possibility is just as interesting as the first."

"That's the squirrely looking kid, isn't it?" asked Al.

Sim confirmed this. "Definitely. Type A student."

"Ah the plot doth thicken," said Al. "If I'm not mistaken, I think he carried a rather large torch for her at Barton's party."

"And she for him?" asked Langstrom.

"She teased him on," I said. "I think he took her seriously, though."

"Alas," said Al in his theatrical way, "the torch kindleth Passion, whose inflamed hand doth turn our heart's desires to ashes."

***

At noon I saw Cambria sitting alone, downcast, in the cafeteria. I stopped by her table to cheer her up. She tried to act chipper, if you can imagine how a sloth might. I sat down opposite her.

"Did you talk to Franky?" I asked.

She nodded. "Yes, he said maybe he didn't see Tasia after all. He said he'd been drinking and was disoriented. He saw somebody he thought was Tasia for a moment, but it was from behind, and now that he thinks about it, she really didn't have the outline of Tasia, and maybe he wasn't near the dorm yet when he saw the person. I can't believe he drank until he was drunk."

"I don't care how much you drink, as long as you're walking and functioning, you should have an idea as to where you're at. Let's face it, nobody was as tipsy as Al and he knew he was in his house. After all, he found the refrigerator."

"I told him where Professor Garfield saw him at eleven thirty, and he said that could be right. After he left Barton's party he got turned around, but then backtracked to the dorm. He couldn't remember well whether he saw the girl he mistook for Tasia before or after he turned around."

Now that I heard the whole explanation, it started to make sense. I remember ending up in a girl's car once just because it had a crumpled hood. It was dark, I had been thirsty, I had quenched my thirst in the only respectable way a young man can, and then there I was, sitting behind the wheel of a car with pink feathers and a picture of Ian Nelson hanging from the rearview mirror. Could happen to anybody with a crumpled hood.

"I think Franky's holding something back," said Cambria, "maybe a lot. It's just plain wrong."

"You think he's our public enemy number one?"

Cambria's lips tightened. "No, can't be," she declared with that tabasco headshake. "There's something we're missing."

I sat there quietly with her. I could see her brain was at work, spinning about. When it came to a full stop, she said, "Tell me abpit upir friends again, but this time everything you know about them, and then I'll tell you all I know about mine."

"What friends of mine?" I asked.

"Well, for starters, Dr. Abbot, Dr. Tate, Dr. Langstrom, and Dr. Garfield. How far do they go back with each other? How did they get to know each other? Where did they go to school? Things like that."

I objected to her identifying Dr. Abbot as a friend, so she rephrased her request, but insisted I give her the low down on all relevant acquaintances at the college. I knew the most about Al and Langstrom, how they went back to high school days and even fooled around together at college before coming here. I explained that Sonia was a local and an arriviste who had licked more boots than a shoeshine boy spat on, which explained why she wanted incriminating evidence against Langstrom, to blackmail him so he wouldn't oppose her candidacy for Professor of the Year. As a bonus, I also gave her a detailed account of Stanley, his childhood and high school years, as well as his abridged college football career.

Cambria didn't look satisfied. "I don't know if we'll get very far with this Robert Jones thing. I think Dr. Abbot is grasping at straws there. Are there any other scandals linked to them? Anything else that would be embarrassing?"

"There was for Langstrom"," I said. "There was some undergrad female drama student after him apparently when he was a grad student, a TA. She ended up getting a boyfriend, but he died in a car wreck. She got mangled. Al said it ruined her hopes for a career, unless she wanted a leading role in *The Witches*."

After I said this, she looked up at me and I spotted a frail but visible ray of hope shimmering in her eyes. "We've got to track down that MM number. Hand it over!"

I took out my phone and gave it to her while she opened up her laptop. She googled, instagrammed, and facebooked about for a while. No result.

She said, "The quickest way to find who the number belongs to is to have the sheriff look it up."

I objected: "Number one, I don't think he would share any information with us if he could trace it, and number two, I don't think he wants to see me without pushing my nose out the back of my head."

"That's a cost I'm willing to take. I'll meet you at five o'clock and we'll go see Dr. Abbot. I think she'll be ready to make a deal."

"No offense, Cambria, but it's just 'no can do.' If Sonia knew that I told you she was actually digging up dirt on Langstrom to blackmail him so she could get Professor of the Year, both of us would find ourselves confined to the interior of an urn and sharing ground with Spot."

She thought about this and saw my point and concluded that I must go into Sonia's lair alone. Having pity on me, she explained to me exactly what I was to say. Having heard her out, I surmised that if Cambria had been Eve back in our garden days, I think she would have given Adam an argument that would have kept them on good terms with the landlord.

***

Despite Cambria's encouraging words and suggestions, I dreaded the hour hand on the wall clock in the adjunct office, as it slowly moved toward the number five. The only thing consoling me was that I doubted the sheriff would be at Sonia's house. November elections were coming up, which meant he had to be driving about, making a high profile of himself so that none could suspect he was holed up at the Bookshire with half a donut sticking out of his mouth.

Sonia welcomed me as if expecting my arrival. We sat down in her parlor, a room with plush carpet, Victorian furniture, and walls lined with old classical leather-bound books that would never be read. For a bit, I suspected a female servant wearing a black dress, white apron, and a little white doily thing on the top of the head would soon arrive with a tray bearing a teapot, two cups and saucers, and an assortment of biscuits. She never materialized.

"You have something for me, I suspect?" she asked.

I dug into my pocket and extricated the card with the MM phone number. "I would like to make a deal," I said.

"One that doesn't include you learning how to wait on tables?"

"As a codicil, perhaps."

"I can make no guarantees but go on."

"I've got two initials and a telephone number that may be of interest to you. They come from Langstrom's phone and the woman who belongs to the initials is into something thick with Langstrom. I don't know what it is, exactly. Maybe an affair. But all I want to know is who the lady is and where she lives."

"And you think my brother can provide you with that information."

"I believe he will provide you with that information, and then I believe you can provide me with that information."

"Let me see the number."

I lifted the card in the air above my head and

out of her reach. "Only if I have your word that I'll get the lady's name and address."

"How do you know it's a lady?"

"Because I called the number."

"And if I don't give you the information you want?"

"Far be it from me to tell the president that you hired me to hack into Langstrom's computer and steal data from his cell phone."

"Yes, it would be far from you to do that." She said this with a raspy voice that was hard to decipher because her clenched teeth restricted the sound waves. She would have made a good understudy for whoever it was who played the leading role in *The Exorcist*. Fortunately, she didn't go to the bother of spinning her head around in a full 360 to glare at me.

"I've already written a letter of confession," I warned her. "Stanley has a sealed copy and it does say clearly on the outside 'Open if Tristan doesn't make it back home alive from Sonia's place tonight.'"

The professor of sociology simmered down a bit, then changed her tune. "I rather like your audacity. We might make a team of it." She drew a breath as if from a cigarette, fully inhaling, then declared, "I don't have a problem sharing information with you. I can't see how it could help Henry. But if ever you threaten me again, you will feel the strong arm of the law, I guarantee it. Even if it's vigilante justice."

"Oh, right," I said. "It's the best justice ever. I swear by it. It's in all the westerns I watch. They rarely get the wrong fellow."

"Good, just so we understand each other. Now, hand over the number."

I did so in rising. She took it sitting down, evincing the shadow of a smile. I'd seen my father make the same grimace. It typically overtook him right before his last move against me on the chessboard and his saying "Checkmate."

There was an intimate silence. She obviously was relishing the moment and I felt rather like I was sitting in the back seat of a car parked along the bluff overlooking the River with two lovebirds seated in front of me in an embrace. One person too many.

I finally felt obliged to make my presence known by asking, "He's too young to have had an affair with Marilyn Monroe, isn't he?"

"Yesss, he is." She drew out the words slowly and softly, one word at a time. "My colleague from that other university, you know, the one with the wife who knew Henry back in the day. I talked to his wife recently and asked her if she remembered any other students associated with Henry when he was a TA. I thought they might know something about Robert Jones. I haven't contacted any yet, but one of the names she gave me was Mavis Marbury."

***

Coming out of Sonia's house injected me with a euphoria no doubt shared with anyone exiting prison after a twenty-year stretch. What I mean to say is that I hadn't suffered much, just like an inmate can't complain of free food and lodging, but the breath of freedom drawn outside overshadowed any inside benefit one could think of.

Dropping into the Batteredmobile, I found my Robin, Cambria, seated beside me and in a stir.

"What did she say?" She asked this repeatedly like a cock who just can't shut off his cockadoodledooer.

I sketched out the salient points and she clapped in personal triumph. "I told you it would work!"

I didn't think Christians were to be proud of themselves and told her as much, but that was a mistake. She lectured me on proper pride and the other kind, selfish pride she called it. But the news I had given her about MM made her curtail her lecture and beat the face of her cell phone with her little thumbs.

"Mavis Marbury," she said after typing in the name and whatever other information she thought pertinent. "She lives in Boston."

"Boston," I said. "That's where Langstrom went to college, at least for his graduate degrees."

Cambria typed some more on her cell phone. "It looks like she's about ten years younger than what I suspect Dr. Langstrom to be. And he might have been about twenty-seven at that time?"

"Well, that Don Juan," I mumbled.

"Did Don Juan go after underage girls?" Cambria asked.

"I don't know if they had underage girls back then, but they sure did when Langstrom was in college."

I started up the Batteredmobile and headed up Holiday Street toward the campus. Cambria asked me to go in the direction of the Bookshire so I could drop her off at the library. I obliged, which allowed me to get a hot caramel latte for the way home.

Once on Highway 67, I listened to One

Direction's "What Makes You Beautiful" and then "Kiss You." The lyrics took me back to high school days and mixed those memories with visions of Cambria, as if she had been there. The thoughts weren't healthy. I knew better than to get mixed up with a religious nut. I suppose some people make it work out, but there would have to be a no-man's land of deep convictions that they would stay out of.

I imagine that would work if only conversing in superficialities. Afterall, the earth's surface is superficial, no one has seen the core, and yet we all live on planet earth together. We could talk weather, Husker football, and missing persons....

"Hmm," I hummed aloud. "It would be problematic. After discussing the weather for five minutes and football for an hour, we'd have to have an acquaintance murdered once every two weeks to live peaceably together the rest of the time, which means we would have to move to Midsomer county."

After class on Friday, Cambria walked back with me to the adjunct office. She told me that one of the things we hadn't done and that we needed to do was to figure out what Tasia was up to. Once we understood that, she claimed, we would know who would have gotten rid of her.

I stood up and looked around at the cubicles behind me to make sure no one could overhear us. The cubicles were empty and bare. Adjuncts, being forever short timers, know better than to decorate their office space with personal items, photos of loved ones, and comical doo-dads.

After seeing that it was all clear, I told Cambria that Tasia's essays didn't reveal much about her and that Jennifer would know more about her than anyone else.

"Didn't you hear them talking together in the dorm late at night or something?" I asked her.

"You mean by eavesdropping?"

"Isn't that what college girls do?"

"That's sexist."

"I'm just saying men are too dull-witted to think of it, too focused on playing video games to have the interest or time."

"I didn't say you were wrong. Just because it's sexist doesn't mean it's false..." Cambria's voice trailed off. "Oh my," she exploded. "Eavesdropping! The laptop, the phone, in Dr. Langstrom's office. That's how she knew you would be at Dr. Abbot's house!"

"You're right!" I said, the scales falling from the eyes. "She must have had the phone or laptop in record mode."

"She's sneaky."

"Not just sneaky," I said. "She plots as well."

"Yes, she works at it."

"What do you mean?"

"When I took her backpack over to Jennifer. You know, the one she left with Franky?"

"Yes."

"While I was taking it over to Jennifer's, I peeked at what was inside."

"Without a warrant?"

"Only the police have to have warrants, except in Midsomer."

"Yes, but they always do mention that they should have one."

"Right, but again, they're police, we're not."

"Point made. So, what did you find?"

"She actually had books in it."

"Surprising for a college student."

"They weren't textbooks, though. And when I got to Jennifer's, I mentioned the books, and Jennifer told me Tasia had other books just like them. She'd seen Tasia reading them from time to time. She took some out of Tasia's nightstand and showed them to me."

"Well, what kind of books were they?"

"They were how-to books. How to analyze people, read their faces, interpret their voice tone, words. How to influence people and win them over to your view."

"Like Carnegie's *How to Win Friends and Influence People*?"

"That may have been one of them. They were dogeared and with notes. And to be honest, now that I think about it, the handwriting in the margins looked a lot like what's on one of the postcards she sent Jennifer, so it must have been Tasia's notes."

"Does Jennifer still have the postcards?"

"No, but she has pics of them on her phone. She said the police took the actual postcards and a couple of Tasia's books. She didn't know why."

I had to take a minute or two to process what Cambria was saying. "So," I finally said, "you discovered that Tasia wasn't the flighty, dumb brunette we had imagined."

"That's right."

"I think we've got enough information to figure out what Tasia was up to."

"And who would have wanted her out of the way!"

After Cambria said this, we decided to write a list of everything we knew about Tasia and people who might have interacted with her. Her trip to Boston, her knowledge of "MM," her relationship with Franky, her books on how to influence people, and her disappearance after Barton's party, these were all pieces to a puzzle, a large one, with many other pieces: The way Angela looked at her from the steps of Neal Hall, the way Sonia dealt with her the night I was found in Sonia's bed, and the way Al looked at her at Barton's party. And then there was the whole "MM" connection: Langstrom arguing with Robert Jones, and Mavis Marbury in an auto accident. The list went on, including details such as the green gum in the door jamb. Eventually we were able to link everything together. We just needed an opportunity to present our case to all involved in order to clear up a few odds and ends.

Once we were done, I told Cambria we needed to investigate the Nebraska City connection. The police never interviewed Franky about Tasia's meeting with a lady in Nebraska City, but obviously Tasia knew someone there. "If you could go up to that coffee shop, I bet you they'd know who the lady is that comes in every morning at six a.m. Go see her and find out what you can."

Cambria agreed. She also told me there were a couple of minor things she had thought of, but they involved a woman's intuition, so she said it wouldn't interest me.

I objected, repeating her claim that we could not keep secrets between us concerning the Tasia affair.

She acquiesced and gave me a clue "as big as the nose in the middle of my face," as she put it. "Stained glass."

"Ah," I said knowingly. "Thank-you."

She rose from her chair and left the adjunct room in search of her Aveo to go up to Nebraska City.

"Stained glass," I mumbled to myself. "I wish I had a woman's intuition."

***

Campus Menace   Preston Shires

The get-together at Sonia's was to take place following the annual Social Sciences Club buffet dinner and meeting at Stickers. The number of people to attend was quite large for our little college. About everyone's in the club, at least everyone majoring in history, political science, sociology, or psychology. Perhaps thirty or so people. The number also included professors from those disciplines.

I arrived early to hand the keys of the Batteredmobile over to Chris. Sonia, one of the faculty who established the club, insisted I sit next to her.

While everyone was chatting, I, as faculty advisor, went to the front of the room and gave a short welcome. Next, the student club president went through the gears, having the secretary read the minutes and the treasurer report on the takings from last year's benefit drives. Meanwhile, I stepped outside to check on my car. It was nowhere in sight. I gave Chris another ten minutes and he still had not shown. I grew impatient, walked a hundred yards or so along the town square in the direction of Sonia's but then thought better of it and made my way back to Stickers to wait at the curb. It took him over half an hour to finally return.

Chris got out of his car with a big smile. Another waiter got out of the passenger's side, showing teeth as well.

"My God," I said, "you appear to think it'll please."

"It matches her house perfectly, I can't see her saying it doesn't," Chris said, dropping the keys in the palm of my hand.

I made it back into the meeting and found cold pizza sitting on my plate.

"I took vegetarian for you," said Sonia. "I didn't think there would be any left by the time you got back. Where'd you go? Out to eat?"

"For a walk, you know, to work up an appetite."

"You were gone long enough to work up two appetites."

"Yes, that allows me to have dessert as well."

"I don't think you'll have time," she said looking at the clock on her cell phone. "You're next on the agenda."

I rose and presented my little fifteen-minute homily on 'Eating Together as Monks'. The title is perhaps more interesting than the subject matter, which discussed how the need for having a communal meal for the Lord's Supper forced hermits to come out of hiding once a week and gather around a table. Of course, eating was obscene by the standards of the day. Swallowing material objects to satisfy the sensual desires of the stomach was unsaintly, so the monks hid their faces from one another as they shoveled in their pound of bread. Anyway, I don't believe I made any members of The Social Sciences Club feel guilty in the least because they finished off dessert while I was finishing my lecture.

Afterwards, the social scientists migrated over to Sonia's house for drinks and socializing. I arrived in their wake, just behind the president of the college, who usually stops by at these functions to mingle with the students, provide uplifting words, and then leave.

I pulled up beside Sonia's house and stared in amazement for a good three or four minutes. Chris had indeed given Sonia a gift as big as her house. Scott toilet paper draped itself up and over the roof from all angles. Spray painted on the lawn in big yellow letters were the words "Worst Professor Award: Sonia Abbot."

President Larimer stood there deciphering the words, a bit like a six-year-old trying to sound out a sentence.

Behind me arrived another car with gyrating lights on top of it. Its occupant descended and marched up to my window with a flashlight glaring angrily at me. I couldn't see much beyond the bright light. The man, (I assumed the torchbearer to be a male), focused on my face for a moment, then uttered a "Hmphhh" of indignation.

He then shifted his flashlight to my back seat. While he did so, I identified the laconic individual as Sheriff Abbot. His left bicep seemed to expand to within an inch of my nose.

I turned about to look at what he was studying and discovered an empty case of Scott toilet paper on my back seat and two apparently empty cans of yellow fluorescent marker paint.

Out of habit he asked me for my driver's license. After looking it over, he said, "Mr. Telsmith, I'm going to ask you to step out of the vehicle. Feel free to resist if you wish."

I suppose that last part of what he said is peculiar to the Southeast Nebraska Handbook for County Sheriffs, because I don't remember hearing it elsewhere. Being completely innocent, I stepped out of the car lightly and asked, "What seems to be the problem, officer?"

I don't quite remember the sequence of events, but I found myself pressed up against my car with my chin on the roof of the Batteredmobile, my legs kicked apart, and my hands knotted together with handcuffs. I was a bit dazed and gauging from the trickle of blood coming from my nose, I had the distinct impression that he may have slammed my face onto the roof of the car before resting my chin upon it.

"I don't believe you're giving me a fair chance to resist," I objected.

He maneuvered me over to the gyrating lights, opened the back door to his vehicle and prepared to toss me in like a bowling ball when I heard my savior's voice.

"Sheriff, this guy didn't tepee the house. He was up at Stickers the whole time. Somebody borrowed his car."

The sheriff loosened his grip on me. Now if it had been Franky coming to save me, I think the sheriff would have just let the bowling ball continue its course, but since it was Stanley, he hesitated.

"How do you know that?"

"Because I was up there. And I don't believe you read him his rights, either. This looks like police brutality to me." Apparently, Stanley came with a coterie of students, because he then asked, "Doesn't it look that way to ya'll who've been filming this?"

There was a consensus among the budding scholars, and I could see A pluses in the offing.

Students don't do nice things for adjuncts for nothing.

"All right, I'm not here to arrest this fool tonight anyway. I can save that for later. Right now, I would appreciate seeing everyone inside the house."

He un-cuffed me and made for the front door.

Stanley came up and patted me on the back. "You owe me a bottle of whiskey," he said.

"Put it on my tab," I said.

Cambria first gave me a hug and then Stanley.

The students and professors, and even President Larimer, were following Sheriff Abbot into the house.

I fell in line but once up on the porch I realized my housemate was not with me. I turned around and saw Cambria discussing something with him. Seemed odd to me. It was a lively discussion with Cambria gesticulating and then finally Stanley nodding affirmatively.

I waited there a minute or two before Cambria joined me up on the porch.

"Stanley isn't coming in?" I asked.

"No," she said, "he's going to run an errand for me."

"What's he getting?"

"A piece of evidence."

"What piece of evidence. I thought we'd discussed everything and had it all worked out."

"Yes, we did, but I want to impress you, so I saved something for last."

We went into the house and entered Sonia's parlor. The chairs were taken, which left some students sitting on the floor. I went into the kitchen and retrieved two more chairs, handing one to Cambria and keeping the other for myself. After we sat down, the sheriff took center stage with the students and faculty seated about him in a circle.

After scanning the audience in Sonia's living room, the sheriff asked, "Which one of you is Cambria Davenport?"

Once Cambria identified herself, he walked over to where she was seated and asked her to produce her cell phone, which she did.

"Now," he said, "call Frank Trotter and tell him to come in here."

"Franky?" asked Cambria weakly.

"Yes."

She executed the call. There was a little negotiating between Cambria and Franky before she persuaded him to come into the house. Apparently, he had been one of our group on the lawn, but had decided not to cross the threshold, and for good reason.

Nevertheless, the door opened and in stepped Franky Trotter, pimples and all.

The sheriff asked to see his driver's license, then gave it back to him, took out his handcuffs and stated, "Mr. Frank Trotter, you are under arrest—"

"Wait a minute!" Cambria stormed over and placed herself between Franky and the Hulk. "He didn't murder Tasia Everett!"

"What?" exclaimed Franky. "Murder?"

"I'm sorry Miss, but you're interfering—"

"Hold on, Steven," Sonia said from across the room. "Let's hear her story."

I had the distinct impression that growing up with Sonia Abbot as your elder sister was a bit like growing up with a prosecutor for a mother. Steven made a motion for Franky to sit down in Cambria's chair.

"You've got the floor, Miss," he said as he placed himself behind Franky, hands on the young man's quivering shoulders.

"Well," said Cambria, "any number of people could have gotten rid of Tasia. Your sister for one."

I looked across the room at Sonia who seemed amused.

Cambria continued the accusations. "Professor Tate or Professor Garfield could have as well."

The sheriff let out a breath of exasperation. "Are you just going to name everyone here without explaining why or how he or she would have killed her?"

"Professor Langstrom," I said, "you could be a suspect too, couldn't you?"

"How so?" Langstrom asked.

"Well, where were you the night Tasia disappeared?"

"I was at home, finishing my grading and getting ready for my bike ride on the morrow. I turned in early."

"Not according to Kaiser."

"Who's Kaiser?" asked the sheriff, taking out a notepad and recording the name.

"Kaiser," Sim explained, "is Henry's German shepherd. And though I wouldn't be surprised if he spoke Deutsch, I didn't know he carried on conversations in English with Tristan."

"Has anybody walked by Professor Langstrom's house, before?" I asked.

Two or three people had done so, one of whom was Barton. "What happens when you walk by, in regard to Kaiser?" I asked.

"Ummm, he barks like crazy."

"No, he doesn't," said Langstrom. "If he barks more than three times, I zap him. Someone should have had an electric collar on Hitler, it would have saved us a lot of grief."

"Only your Kaiser," I observed, "is smarter than Hitler would have been, because Kaiser has figured out that if he barks when you're not home, nothing happens. Cambria and I were walking by your house late on Midterm Party Night and Kaiser started barking when we got within sight of your house and kept barking until we were out of sight. You, Langstrom, were not there."

The sheriff jotted down what I had said and then asked Langstrom, "So, where were you?"

"Damn!" said Langstrom. "Man's best friend, my eye."

"Where were you?" repeated Sheriff Abbot.

"I was at my office at the college. I'm sure my computer history will verify that I was there."

"What were you doing there?" the sheriff insisted.

"I was grading papers and it took longer than expected. You see, I wanted to get through all the exams, and I knew if I stayed home, it might take even longer, because I might be visited."

"By whom?"

"Al or Sim or both. We normally get together on Midterm Party Night. I had told them we wouldn't, but, no offense boys," he said looking in their direction, "but I didn't trust either of you, and given a choice between reading student essays and having drinks with my pals, I was afraid I might succumb to temptation. And not being a believer, there's no forgiveness for it."

Sheriff Abbot finished jotting down Langstrom's story. He held his right hand up in the air in a gesture commanding everyone to keep silent. "Now," he said, "what I've gathered is that Henry Langstrom told his friends he was staying at home on the night of Friday, nine October. In reality, Henry Langstrom went to his office at the college. Where exactly?"

"Neal Hall, room 204," said Langstrom.

"...at room 204, Neal Hall," said the sheriff as he included it in his notes. "What time did you go to your office and at what time did you return from it?"

Langstrom answered quickly. "At eight p.m. I went up to the office, and I came back around midnight."

"Did anyone see you?"

"I don't know, but as I said, the computer saw me."

"Right," said the sheriff.

"And you, Tristan Telsmith and Cambria Davenport, together you walked past Henry Langstrom's residence at eleven p.m. You didn't cross each other, notice each other, you two and the professor?

"No," I said.

"None of those interviewed who were at the party reported seeing Tasia Everett after eleven p.m. My suspicion is that the woman calling herself Tasia Everett disappeared sometime between eleven and eleven thirty-five p.m. By eleven thirty-five, Miss Everett's phone was shut off."

The sheriff then looked back at Cambria. "It's pretty easy to verify the professor's story, so I think you'll need something a little more concrete to exonerate your friend Frank Trotter, because I've got some pretty damning evidence against him."

Having heard this, Franky started to protest but then dropped his head as if he were Henry VIII's latest wife awaiting the axeman.

"First," said Cambria in her I'm-taking-charge voice, "before you arrest Franky, or anybody else for that matter, you've got to establish what Tasia was up to. Then you'll have motive."

"And what was Miss Everett, as you knew her, up to?" asked the sheriff.

"Well, we can figure it out by her behavior. For example, on the night of the president's party, Tasia told your sister that her house had been broken into, and then she and Barton accompanied her to the house, this house. The two of them waited around for your sister to discover the intruder. Is that not right, Barton?"

Barton agreed and Cambria continued by saying, "Your sister discovered the intruder. It was Tristan Telsmith, right Professor Telsmith?"

I nodded.

"But," Cambria said, "Dr. Abbot told Tasia it was you, Sheriff Abbot, who was in the house."

"What does that even prove?" asked the sheriff. "It's not evidence of anything. I have evidence. Hard evidence against Mr. Trotter. We found a crowbar stashed in the bottom of a trash can down at the car wash with the victim's blood on it. And you know what else was on it?"

"Yes," said Cambria, crossing her arms. "Franky Trotter's fingerprints."

"Oh..." responded the sheriff, surprised.

"Because silly Franky Trotter is obsessed with Tasia Everett and for an understandable reason: she made him believe she loved him and then she seduced him and dumped him."

"Well, now you're helping out my case. He has motive." He said this while happily jotting down what she had said into his notebook.

"No, he had love on his mind. He took the crowbar down to the Langdon Bridge Car Wash and attempted to break into the change machine to get enough money to buy concert tickets to One Direction for himself and Tasia Everett! Isn't that right, Franky?"

We witnessed a gentle nod from the bowed head of the condemned. "I heard Barton say it could be done, but those machines are like Fort Knox."

"Hey," said Barton, looking at the sheriff, "I was just jokin', it's the way I am, that's all."

The sheriff ignored Barton and turned on Cambria, "You're protecting Mr. Trotter. Obsessed, love-sick people kill the one who spurns them all the time."

"No, you just don't understand Tasia Everett yet. I'll bet all the toilet paper on this house that Tasia Everett said to your sister something about how hard it might be to get Professor of the Year while sleeping with an adjunct, namely Tristan Telsmith."

The sheriff stiffened at Cambria's words, his hands squeezing poor Franky's boney shoulders.

"Surely one's private affairs, so to speak," said Sim, "have no bearing on one's capacity to teach. Isn't that right Dr. Larimer?"

The president of the college who had been quietly observing the proceedings now coughed gently and said, "Dr. Abbot is an esteemed professor as are the others in this room. I don't know yet who will be awarded Professor of the Year, but like I say, there are many worthy candidates. There is a committee mixed of faculty and deans involved in the election, if you will. Dean Vickers coordinates this, but I'm well aware of the work she and the others put into it. They look at a variety of things. Student evaluations are indeed helpful, but so are classroom observations conducted by the various deans. I would be well pleased and not surprised if any one of you were awarded the prize."

Sim chuckled. "I love politicians. That's why I teach political science. Only a politician can give an answer five times longer than the question and end up saying nothing. Let me put it this way. How many professors awarded the prize in the past had anything remotely scandalous attached to their name? None, zero, because we must protect the reputation of the college, because if we don't, parents won't want to send their precious little boys and girls here and we'll lose money. I could be the most beloved professor on campus, but if I get caught shoplifting a cookie at the Bookshire, I'm suddenly the last name on the list of candidates. Sorry, Sonia."

Sonia started to answer but Cambria cut her off.

"Like I said," Cambria said forcefully, "Tasia let Dr. Abbot know that she knew something about her and Professor Telsmith."

"Watch what you're saying Miss," said the sheriff. I seconded the sheriff.

"No, Steven," Sonia said. "I think I know where she's going with this. Explain yourself, Cambria."

"Tasia had two obsessions. The first one was messing with people. That's what she was doing with Franky, she just wanted to upend his life. She liked to see others fail and suffer."

"Why would she do that?" asked Angela.

"People who have succumbed to sin want to see others fail as well."

Angela rolled her eyes.

"It's just human nature," said Cambria. "If they succeed, they don't feel as much of a failure in their own eyes, but, it's a horrible crime to cause the innocent to stumble."

"Ah, yes, it's the old millstone story," said Al with a wave of the hand in Franky's direction. "'Better for her that a millstone were hanged about her neck, and she cast into the sea, than that she should offend one of these little ones.'"

"Or did that have something to do with

baptism?" asked Sim.

"You may mock," said Cambria, "but this particular sin that threatens us all had an especial hold on Tasia. It's what motivated her to come here the other night when Professor Telsmith was in the house. She knew he was going to be here, so she sprung the trap to have him arrested, humiliated, and perhaps jobless."

"Whoa!" said Sheriff Abbot. "How would she know Tristan was coming here?"

"You tell him, Professor Telsmith. You know what happened!" said Cambria.

21

As all eyes shifted to me, I remembered reading once that upon the death of President Franklin Delano Roosevelt, the vice president of the United States, Harry Truman, said, "I felt like the moon, the stars, and all the planets had fallen on me." I would have easily traded places with him.

Not being one to shirk duty, however, especially when in view of the college president, I rose from my chair like Perry Mason would have, if he could have, and addressed the jury with the following words:

"It all has to do with the laptop, the phone, and Dr. Langstrom's office. A few weeks ago, Tasia left her laptop bag in Dr. Langstrom's office. She manipulated Janitor Dovich into letting her back in when Langstrom, Al, and Sim were out of the office so she could retrieve her laptop and phone. She did not want them finding her phone. Why? Because she was using it to record their conversation."

"Oh, goodness," said Al. "I hope that wasn't the day I was discussing laxatives, was it, Henry?"

"Yes, you were running on about it."

"What was she up to?" asked the sheriff.

"She was fishing for any embarrassing information she could catch concerning any one in Langstrom's office. When she listened to her recording, she heard about your guys' plan," I said looking at Henry, Al, and Sim. "Would you be willing to tell everyone what it was?"

"We defer to you," said Langstrom.

"Okay," I said, "but I do feel like something of a Judas."

"No, no," said Langstrom, almost encouragingly. "We're never going to pay you thirty pieces of silver."

"All right, I will tell it and for two reasons: First, because I think it necessary to do so to protect the innocent; and second, because the sheriff already knows about it. The plan was to send me into Sonia's house to get information off her computer."

"Well," said Sim, "all's fair in love and war. We know Sonia would have done as much for any one of us, if one of us had been in the running for Professor of the Year. In fact, I bet you she would have to confess, if under oath, that she has hatched a plot just as devious."

"Point well taken, Sim," said Sonia nervously, fearing that Sim knew of her attempt to have me hack Langstrom's computer, and hoping he wouldn't elaborate if he did.

"So, Cambria," the sheriff said, taking the focus off his sister, "what, according to you, happened to Tasia's little plan to humiliate Tristan Telsmith."

"Well, as I indicated, she planned on witnessing Professor Telsmith's arrest, just for the joy of it. But that, as you know, is not what happened because Dr. Abbot covered for Professor Telsmith and told Tasia and Barton they could leave. That's when Tasia saw an opportunity to indulge in her second obsession."

"And what was this second obsession?"

"Blackmail, of course. It's true that Tasia appeared to be a ditzy, pretty girl, but in reality, she was a calculating and somewhat brilliant blackmailer. That's why she got rid of Barton right after Sonia said it was just her brother upstairs."

"Yeah," said Barton. "She said she was tired and was heading back to the dorm."

"But actually," continued Cambria, "she

went to hide in the hedge. She wanted to make sure it was Professor Telsmith who came out of the house and not you, Sheriff. Once verified, she drew the conclusion that the reason Dr. Abbot didn't say it was Professor Telsmith upstairs was because she and he were having an affair."

Sonia approached her brother. "I think she's got the right of it. Tasia asked me, 'Can someone get Professor of the Year if she's sleeping around?' I told her, 'Why not, it's still teaching.'"

The sheriff glanced darkly at me.

"You know," I said, the voice wavering ever so slightly, "that's not what was going on, as was stated, I was hacking into Sonia's computer, or at least trying to."

The sheriff, returning to his notebook, shifted his attention back to Cambria. "Go on."

"Well, I'll have to go out on a limb here, but I'd like to ask Jennifer to open Tasia's purse and dump its contents on the coffee table."

Jennifer explained that Cambria had asked her to bring Tasia's purse with her. Cambria walked over to the table and lifted up a little packet, opened it and showed everyone what it was: A piece of green chewing gum.

"Does this look familiar, Professor Telsmith?"

"Yes, green chewing gum had been jammed into the lock hole of Langstrom's office door."

"That," said Cambria, "was Tasia's doing. Why? Because she wanted to snoop inside Professor Langstrom's office. And she did, thanks to the gum, which prevented the door from locking. She simply stuffed it into the door lock hole after one of her advising sessions and waited. Once she saw her chance, she slipped inside, found his phone, and went through the address book. What struck her was that every phone number corresponded to a full name, such as 'Sim Garfield,' except one number. That number corresponded to just two letters: MM."

When Cambria said "MM" Langstrom sat up straight as if an ill-tempered cat had been dropped in his lap.

Cambria continued, "Tasia, being very sharp, recognized that Dr. Langstrom didn't want anyone knowing who this person was, therefore, something scandalous was very likely connected to that name."

"How would you know I had an 'MM' in my address book?" he asked aggressively. "Have you been looking at my phone too? Besides," he said, taking out his phone and scrolling down the list of names in the address book, "there is no MM." He got up, walked over to Sheriff

Abbot and practically shoved the phone in his face. "See?"

"You could have erased it," observed the sheriff.

Cambria picked up where she left off when Langstrom sat back down. "The real question is 'How is Mavis Marbury linked to Robert Jones?'"

"Robert Jones?" asked the sheriff.

"Interesting," I said, "apparently Sonia didn't fill you in."

"I still don't know much about Robert Jones," said Sonia, "thanks to your lack of computer hacking skills."

Cambria disagreed. "You know Jones was timid, unbecoming, but witty and always dressed to the nines. Perhaps gay. He also had an argument with Dr. Langstrom, a TA back then, out in a parking lot of the university cafeteria at Boston. He asked you, Dr. Langstrom, 'Have you no sense of decency,' as if he were in the McCarthy hearings. All that information has been handed down to us second, or even third hand from some thirty years ago, I suppose, so it can't be all too accurate, but does it ring a bell, Dr. Langstrom?"

There was an all-round silence. Finally,

Langstrom said, "Yes, we had the argument and he was all those things you say, but he wasn't gay."

"As you were an eyewitness," said Cambria, "we thank you for correcting that, but what, then, was his connection to Mavis Marbury."

"He was dating Mavis. And I suppose if I had an 'MM' in my phone's address book, it could have stood for her, but I didn't have her number."

"And what happened to Robert Jones? Where is he?" asked Sonia.

"He died in a car accident. It was years ago, when Mavis was a student of mine, when I taught at Boston."

"And she was disfigured in the accident, wasn't she?" I said.

"Yes," said Al.

"She was only fit to play a role in *The Witches*, wasn't she Al?"

"Oh," he said, "she would be perfect."

"And why," I asked, "upon hearing the name of Mavis Marbury did your brain connect her to the film *The Witches*?"

"You just have to take a look at her," he said unashamedly, spreading his hands apart as if this were self-evident.

"No," I said, "it's because you subconsciously

connected her name to your play entitled *The Bewitched*."

"I'm afraid I don't follow," said Sheriff Abbot, twiddling his pen.

"It was a Freudian slip," I explained. "Al identifies Mavis Marbury with his play, *The Bewitched*, but he doesn't want anyone to know that, but when he wanted to make a tasteless joke about Mavis's disfigured face, he instinctively named another story with a very similar title, *The Witches*."

Al set his jaw and dropped his nonchalance. No one appreciates being analyzed.

Sim commented, "Have you switched from being Maxwell Smart to being Sigmund Freud?"

Al piled on, "There's one thing we know about Freud, now: he was bonkers, as is your convoluted theory about me associating *The Bewitched* with *The Witches*, two completely different stories." He paused, took a deep breath, and continued on less stridently. "I see no connection between Mavis Marbury and *The Bewitched*, albeit I think I could use her as one of the Habsburgs in my play, of course that's if Cambria declines the role." He looked over at the sheriff. "You see, I promised her first."

I felt obliged to comment. "I have nothing against a person who has had a misfortune and become disfigured. It could happen at any time to any one of us. But as things stand now, I can't see the logic in replacing Cambria with a blemished actress. Physically speaking, Cambria is far from flawed."

I heard an emotional "Ahhhh" in the crowd that had just enough mockery in it to tell me it came from Sim. Of course, this opened the floodgates to some giggling and snickering.

I was suddenly very self-conscious, and I awkwardly turned my head, rather jerkily, toward Cambria. She, majestic chin and all, looked dreamily at me with rosy cheeks and teary eyes.

"Uh humm," I said in clearing my throat to regain some composure; then, in as manly a voice as I could muster, I stated, "Tasia found out about 'MM,' Mavis Marbury."

"Yes," said Cambria quickly, equally anxious to reestablish the conversation, "and she contacted her."

This bit of news erased the snickering and giggling.

"What?" said Langstrom, acting surprised.

"Tasia found out about Mavis Marbury and contacted her," Cambria repeated.

"Why would Mavis have anything to do with Tasia?" asked Langstrom. "It makes no sense."

"Ask Al," said Cambria. "He'll know why."

"I'm sorry to disappoint," responded Al.

"Then I'll take away your disappointment by enlightening you," said Cambria. "As we said before, Tasia was not some feeble-minded beauty pageant contestant. She did her homework on 'MM'—"

"Oh, that would be a first." Al said, interrupting Cambria. "So now she's a scholar?"

"You know what I'm getting at," said Cambria. "Tasia found out where Mavis lived, where she had gone to college, who her professors had been. She knew something was up between you and her."

"What?" Al exploded. "I don't need a little Bible thumper making accusations. You see sin everywhere, but only because your damned religion won't let you enjoy it. But it just may be that nobody's sinning, that it's okay to get blind drunk and make love with whoever's willing."

Cambria was shocked by Al's explosion. "I'm just trying to establish what happened so an innocent person doesn't pay for somebody else's crime. This whole Tasia affair is about Mavis Marbury and Robert Jones and has nothing to do with Franky Trotter. That's what I want to prove."

Al calmed down a bit and asked Cambria,

"So you're saying I had a to-do with Mavis because the initials MM were found in Henry's phone?"

"No," I said. "That's not it."

Cambria looked at me, wondering whether I'd jumped ship.

"No," I repeated, waiting to gather my thoughts. Al's outburst had lit a lightbulb in my brain. Cambria and I had concluded both Langstrom and Al had dispensed with Tasia, but now I saw differently.

"What kind of car do you drive, Al?" I asked.

"Car? Why a Lincoln Navigator, an SUV."

"Exactly the same car Henry drives."

"Same model, yes."

"The two of you are peas in a pod, if one gets a Lincoln Navigator, so does the other. If one gets a Samsung phone, so does the other. Because both of you leave your phones on Henry's desk to go to lunch—"

"I'm sorry," interrupted Henry, "but you're wrong there."

I was stumped by his reprimand.

"How so?" asked Cambria.

"I always put mine in my drawer. You've never noticed, Tristan?"

"Wow!" I exclaimed. "No, I hadn't, but that only confirms what I'm thinking." Turning to Al,

I said, "Both Tasia and I had picked up your phone, Al, thinking it was Henry's. Could we have a look at your phone's address book?"

"I don't have it on me."

"Do you want Langstrom here to dial your number?" I asked.

Al's dropping of the jaw gave away his fib. "Okay," he said, "Mavis and I had a fling back in the day, before the accident. I didn't want to broadcast it because, well," he looked sheepishly over at Langstrom, "other people may have been seeing her at the same time."

"It wasn't as secret as you thought," said Langstrom. "I think everyone knew, certainly my wife knew about you and Mavis. And I didn't care, which is why I never brought it up."

"I wish you would have brought it up," said Al. "Anyway, Mavis, hearing that I'm still single, wanted to meet up again, and kept calling me. I'm not totally callous, I returned her calls, so I might have Mavis's number, but that doesn't mean anything."

"It meant something to Tasia," Cambria said. "Tasia went to Nebraska City to not only find out about Mavis, but also to go see her if necessary, even if it meant taking the plane. She met Patricia Langstrom in a coffee shop there. The barista knows Patricia as a regular customer and remembers her meeting with a young woman matching Tasia's description. I dropped in on Mrs. Langstrom this afternoon and she told me all about her encounter with Tasia. Tasia heard about an auto accident Mavis Marbury and Robert Jones were in, and she found out that both were in a class with you, back when you were a TA in Boston, teaching drama. Your soon-to-be-ex, Dr. Langstrom, told Tasia all the sordid details about your relationship with Mavis and Professor Tate's as well."

"I think you give my wife too much credit," said Langstrom. "She may have been a looker once upon a time, but she was never well informed about me."

"Trust me," said Cambria, "a woman always knows what other women are up to in matters of love. Right Angela?"

Cambria surprised Angela by calling on her.

"I'm sorry?" responded Angela.

"Tell me," Cambria asked, "have you noticed any women paying attention to Professor Telsmith?"

"Why would you ask me that?"

"Because I sure notice the way you look at him."

"Well," Angela said looking at me. "I can't

help it if Tristan and I have feelings for each other, it's not a crime."

I was flabbergasted. I thought Angela was sweet on Stanley. I certainly wasn't attracted to her.

"So," reiterated Cambria, "did you notice any other women paying attention to Professor Telsmith?"

"I think you pay a lot of wasted attention on him, if that's what you mean. And Tasia, was, of course, hopelessly in love with him."

There was a perceptible measure of bitterness and disdain in Angela's remarks, and I'm afraid I not only looked rather dumbfounded listening to these revelations, but I could also feel the hot blood rising to my cheeks. I was hit by a royal dizzy spell with the room spinning about, but I managed to soldier on like an American GI. I didn't want to end up like one of those blokes in the Queen's Guard who comes to 'order arms' and then falls flat on his face.

"You see what I'm saying Dr. Langstrom," I could hear Cambria say, "women notice these things."

I lost track of the rest of the conversation for a moment or two, wondering why Cambria didn't contradict Angela. Sure, Cambria and I agreed to an armistice for the sake of solving Tasia's murder, but I didn't think she could have any positive feelings toward me after our falling out.

Al's voice brought me out of my contemplation as I heard him say to Cambria, "Even if Patricia, Henry's soon to be 'ex', filled Tasia in on Mavis and Robert, she wouldn't have told her anything more than what we already know, Henry and I."

"But then Tasia did find out more," said Cambria. "Using the leads Mrs. Langstrom gave her, Tasia made a trip out to Boston and back in order to have coffee with Mavis and coax some information out of her. Information that would be compromising for you, Professor Tate. Do you know what that information was?"

"Enlighten me, but you're going to have to use your supernatural connections because, for starters, you haven't talked to Tasia, and for enders, there is no compromising information."

"You said a moment ago that you would put Mavis in your play, *The Bewitched*, did you not?"

"Everybody heard it, but I still have a preference for you."

"Well, the truth of the matter is that *The Bewitched* is *not* your play."

"You're going to have to get yourself another fictional God because that revelation is totally false!"

"It isn't false," declared Cambria. "The play was written by Robert Jones. He asked you to look it over because he trusted you and respected your opinion. And you did look it over, and you recognized it for what it was: a timeless masterpiece. Then he unexpectedly died, and you profited from his death. You kept the play, waited for three decades, and then published it under your own name. That's what Tasia found out!"

"Most certainly not, but I'll give you an A+ for creative fiction."

"I'm sure there's a fifty-fifty deal of some sort that Tasia worked out with Mavis. And that's why Tasia came to see you on Midterm Party Night. To collect the money, a large sum of money for her and Mavis, so that they would keep quiet and you could keep your job. What's more, you're probably the one who suggested to her to come disguised, so nobody would suspect there was anything going on between you two. But the reality is that you didn't want anyone knowing she was coming to your house so you could safely dispose of her!"

The room went silent. It all sounded so

feasible. Everyone's eyes were upon the sheriff.

"I'm afraid there's the little issue of the crowbar," said the sheriff. "You've spun a nice story, Cambria, made a lot of people nervous, but we've got concrete evidence linking Franky to what is most probably the murder weapon."

I think my father's spirit took over my movements at that moment because I found myself, like a defense lawyer, walking over to Franky. Standing beside him, I said directly to Sheriff Abbot, "The blood of Tasia Everett was on the crowbar handled by Frank Trotter because it already had her blood on it when he got ahold of it. Where did he find it? Franky stole it. Where did he steal it from? From the garage of Alfred Tate."

"Well then," said Al, "someone must have bashed her over the head and then stuck it in my garage."

"I don't think that's the way it happened," said Cambria. "I think what happened is that on Midterm Party Night, Alfred Tate, after being dropped off by Tristan, looked up Tasia's phone number that was scribbled into his book by Sophocles, called her to confirm that she was on her way, then, crowbar in hand, waited outside for her to show up to receive her first payment, but it was a cosh rather than cash."

"Outside my house?"

"Yes, that's when you heard Sonia talk of the crematorium. You had to be outside, because inside, with jazz playing, no one hears anything."

"I was too drunk to be maneuvering about outside, laying quietly in ambush, and neatly delivering a targeted blow to the head."

"Too drunk?" asked Cambria incredulously. "According to an eyewitness report," she said glancing at me, "you walked through your living room without running into furniture, tossed a book deftly onto the coffee table, grabbed a water bottle from the fridge, and then suddenly relapsed into drunkenness only when you realized Tristan Telsmith was watching you from his car. Then, as you yourself indicated, you sat down with a book. You were no more drunk than I am."

"But," Sim intervened on Al's behalf, "no one saw Tasia that night anywhere near Al's house."

"Yes, even you did, Professor Garfield," Cambria told him, "you and Franky. Franky saw her from behind. He sensed it was her because of her height and the way she walked, but he wasn't totally sure. He was afraid to catch up with her, because, on the one hand, he thought maybe it wasn't her, and, on the other, because she had ignored him at the party. He wanted to approach her with the concert tickets in hand."

"How do you explain that I saw her?" asked Sim.

"Snowdrift," I said. "It's like two people seeing a snowdrift from different points of view. To one it's three feet tall, to the other, at the far end of it, it's six feet tall."

He was not alone in looking completely confused, so I said, "Let me explain: Tasia was wearing Jennifer's gym clothes to disguise herself, to make herself look frumpy. She's an actress. But because she did not know Franky was behind her, she walked like herself, like a pretty girl. Then, when she came head on with you and your dog, seeing you in the distance, she walked like a man. Her dark complexion made you think she was a young Hispanic high schooler."

"Come to think of it," said Sim, rubbing his brow thoughtfully, "you're right, it was her, but she looked exactly like I described her."

"Yes, and she probably continued walking along like a young man all the way to Al's house. What she didn't count on was that Al would be waiting for her in the hedge. The crowbar did the rest."

"I was home in bed!" exclaimed Al.

Cambria turned to the sheriff, "You did find Professor Tate's fingerprints on the crowbar as well, did you not?"

"Yes, but that's only natural as he identified it as his own, and," he concluded with his voice trailing off as he realized how weak his evidence sounded, "Franky's were superimposed on his."

"Of course, they would be," said Cambria.

"But how would he come by the crowbar?" asked the sheriff.

"Dr. Tate leaves his garage open all the time. Most everyone in town probably knows what he's got in there."

Cambria then walked over to the side door. She put her fingers upon the handle and asked Sonia, "Are all the houses on this street designed the same way?"

"Pretty much, why?"

"Because if they all have basements like yours, I may have a surprise for you all."

Having said this, she opened the door and in stumbled Tasia, forced into the room from behind by Stanley, who held her up with one hand while holding a copy of Sophocles' *Antigone* in the other. We all looked at her agape. Tasia had a strange, indifferent look about her. Her eyes were glazed over, and standing before us she gently swayed back and forth.

Lifting up the book he said, "I found this on Professor Tate's coffee table, and it has Tasia's phone number on the last page."

"And Tasia?" I asked.

"She was in Professor Tate's basement. Just like Cambria said she would be."

"She's a criminal!" cried out Al. "She's a menace to the campus, to everyone! Her real name is Anna Winthrop and she's wanted in Canada for kidnapping, blackmail, and corruption of a minor. I was going to release her tomorrow morning. I just needed the drugs to wear off, now that I could blackmail her back."

"Canadian?" said Sim doubtfully. "I didn't think Canadians did things like that."

"Canadian?" repeated Sheriff Abbot. "That's why we couldn't trace the fingerprints."

"But what of Mavis," exclaimed Langstrom. "She could still blackmail you!"

"I can handle her; I've seduced her once. I can do it again, it's not like the witch has men trotting after her." He stood there, his chest heaving with anger, then he added, "And I just about had Mavis in my corner again before this despicable...." He looked hard at Tasia, and then leapt toward her with his hands outstretched to grasp her around the throat.

Stanley, dropping *Antigone*, delivered a blow that sent Al straight to the floor.

The sheriff whipped out his phone and ordered a fire and rescue squad to the scene to attend to Tasia. Then he looked at Stanley and said, "Mr. umm—"

"Just call me Stanley."

"Yes, Stanley," the sheriff said as he went over to take Tasia over to a couch to sit her down, "make sure Dr. Tate doesn't move."

"I think that's already been taken care of," said Sim, looking down upon his friend.

President Larimer had risen by this time and was calling the college security and medical personnel to come to the house.

I took Cambria by the arm and walked her toward the front door to get out of everyone's way.

"How did you know where she was?" I asked.

"The basement windows we saw in the back of Professor Tate's yard. They had a faux stained glass covering. Why would he do that, I thought, unless, he did not want someone seeing who was down there? And his constant playing of music. It would cover any sounds Tasia might make. It was a guess, but my intuition told me it was going to be the right one."

I had to admit she did impress me. I mean I

would put faux stained glass on my bedroom window just to keep nosy young women from looking in and telling me to clean up, so Al's colored glass didn't surprise me at all. As I congratulated her upon her acumen, I noticed she lacked the smug look Poirot exhibited after saving an innocent from the clutches of the Scotland Yard and revealing the villain to be the least suspected of all.

"What's with the downturned lips?" I asked.

She lifted her face and said, "I almost feel sorry for Tasia."

"Why? If I were her, I'd be on my knees thanking you for saving me from an interminable diet of trumpets and saxophones and throaty singers."

"If it hadn't been for us," Cambria noted, "she would probably have walked free tomorrow. She couldn't have blackmailed Professor Tate anymore, but she wouldn't have been going to jail. Now, both Professor Tate and Tasia are going to be locked up."

She had a point. I looked over at Al and Tasia. Al was just pouting, but Tasia, from her recumbent position, was looking at Cambria from underneath the eyebrows, chin down, eyes up and glaring. That sort of look.

"I see what you mean," I said.

"Our intent was good," Cambria said philosophically, "and that matters. And one can never tell with God. He always surprises. Sometimes, it's the worst day of our life that transforms us into someone better. It happened to me."

I felt like maybe I should ask her what her worst day was, it's hard to imagine anyone getting the best of Cambria, even God, but at that moment the fire and rescue siren stole our attention.

Cambria instinctively opened the front door and we both went out onto the porch. Seeing the flashing lights approaching, we hurried down to the sidewalk to direct the men toward the right house.

Satisfied, I turned to Cambria and observed that she still bore upon her countenance that solemn philosophical expression.

"Oh, Cambria," I said entreatingly, "you needn't be so melancholy. It's much better this way than if we'd done nothing at all. If it weren't for us, Tasia would just move on to her next victim and Al onto his next victim. Think of it that way. We saved John Doe and Jane Doe of the future from getting blackmailed and cheated."

Looking down at her, I believe I detected a softening of the face, a relaxing of that jaw of hers.

"Let's take a walk down toward the levee," I

suggested. "In all honesty I think we did a bang-up job."

Her face brightened a bit.

"Well, given our method," she said cheerily enough as we began our promenade, "we were bound to get to the facts of the case."

"How so?"

"You don't know?" she asked.

"Good God, no." I said.

"Well, since you put it in those terms, I can tell you. We gathered our facts from people who had heard about Robert Jones, second and third hand information perhaps, but corroborated by an eyewitness. So, even if Robert Jones died thirty years ago, the story about his parking lot altercation with Henry Langstrom was verified, as was his McCarthy-like exclamation."

"Yes," I said. "It certainly established that Langstrom and Jones knew each other, and because the argument was out in the open and Langstrom didn't deny it, it suggested that their squabble was over a girl and nothing more serious."

Cambria nodded and continued, "You also mentioned Robert Jones's personal characteristics: his timidity and cleverness, etcetera. I noted that you did not use the exact words from our source. You used synonyms, but it didn't matter because Dr. Langstrom agreed they were correct."

"And," I added, "knowing what kind of a person Robert Jones was, principally timid but clever, and a drama student, made him a good candidate for writing an outstanding play."

"However," Cambria noted, "Dr. Langstrom did remark that our one speculation concerning Robert Jones, that he was gay, was false. I'm sure Dr. Tate and others would have told us the same thing. In other words, we see that the eyewitnesses would not let false assumptions persist."

"And this reinforced the idea that Robert Jones and Mavis Marbury were an item, something Langstrom and Al knew all along."

A cool breeze out of the northwest began to pick up, and instinctively we walked closer together, side by side. "And then," Cambria said, "you pointed out how both Franky and Dr. Garfield saw the same person, Tasia, walking down the street, but each from a different perspective, which led them to describe her differently, but truthfully."

"Right," I said, "and because of this we were able to establish that Tasia was on her way to Al's place."

"You know what I'm getting at, Tristan, don't

you?" She stopped walking after she asked this question, and so did I. She looked up at me and asked, "You don't mind me calling you Tristan since you allow that Angela girl to call you that, do you?"

"No, I've probably got a split personality anyway: sometimes the scholar in search of answers, sometimes just me."

"I can't say I dislike either."

"I feel you stray from the subject at hand, Cambria."

"Yes, you're right. So, again, you know what I'm getting at, don't you, Tristan?"

"That I never should have said 'Good God, no.'"

"Exactly, because people reporting on an event from different perspectives will give different accounts and yet they will be equally true. Just like one person's account of an event in Matthew will differ from another person's account of the same event in Luke. And even though Robert Jones died thirty years ago, eyewitnesses are still alive to give us a first-hand account, just like Luke and the others had eyewitness reports. And Dr. Langstrom, an eyewitness, was able to verify and correct the account we had, just like the hundreds of eyewitnesses of Jesus' ministry could verify and correct anything being reported to Matthew, Mark, or Luke. And we had our scribe there, Sheriff Abbot, writing down what the witnesses said. He read back, at one point, what he had taken down. We agreed with his record. And if tonight you write down your own account, it will differ in style and vocabulary from his, but not in content. Like Matthew and Mark, Sheriff Abbot's and Tristan Telsmith's accounts will both be true."

I must confess that her words troubled me. It's not that my arguments against the reliability of Scripture were not valid, it's that her arguments appeared to be equally valid. In other words, intellectually and historically, one can legitimately argue both that Jesus never rose from the dead and that he did. So, it leaves us with a choice, an act of faith. I have put all my faith in the former argument, but I could shift my allegiance, I suppose, and place all my faith in the second argument.

It's as if Cambria read my thoughts as I pondered where to place my trust.

"If you remain the denier," she said, "you'll be your own god, alone in the universe, without purpose, drifting. Apparently that doesn't bother us when we're young and discovering the world, but once we reach a certain age and the world becomes known to us, loneliness and purposelessness will eat away at us, but by then, we'll be so firmly committed to denial that our pride won't let us believe. Just know that if you embrace the existence of God now, you won't be alone, his Spirit will come upon you, you'll be forever comforted, you'll know him firsthand."

We walked up to the top of the levee and sat down on the grass and looked up into the vast heavens with their constellations spread across the night sky and tried to discern the galaxies far beyond. How insignificant I am, and yet, from whence comes this sense of wanting to be someone, of wanting to be content, of wanting to be forever, of wanting to be forever content? Has Nature made me this way, or am I the begotten of Someone greater?

The End

AUTHOR'S NOTE

I once wrote a critique of Bart Ehrman's book *Misquoting Jesus*, which claims to prove the unreliability of Scripture. Reading over my small tome, however, I became quickly bored, set it aside, and read an entertaining mystery instead. Then it dawned on me: Why not work some of my objections to Ehrman's book into a novel, make them palatable?

In *Campus Menace*, I think I succeeded. Although the mystery is front and center, a few, but certainly not all, of my objections to Ehrman's claims make their way into the storyline.

I accomplished this by placing the mystery in a college town, where debates about religion and politics are common fare. I want to say, however, that Aspinwall College, its students and faculty, and even the town of Aspinwall, are mostly fictitious. The characters are not based on any of my colleagues, past or present. The context, however, reflects the typical setting one might find at one or more of the institutions I've taught at.

I wrote "mostly fictitious" rather than "all fictitious" because the river town of Aspinwall did exist once upon a time back in the 1860s and 1870s. It died, like so many other short-lived frontier settlements, when the railroad ignored it.

In my story, Aspinwall survives to the present. The other towns and thoroughfares mentioned in Nemaha County, Nebraska, within which Aspinwall is situated, do exist. So, if you do come visit our pleasant land of rolling hills, timbered vales, and grain fields, you'll already be familiar with the roads and villages for having read this book. However, don't try to take the Langdon Bridge over the Missouri, as it belongs to fictional Aspinwall.

Preston Shires

More about the Author and His Books

When I was a sophomore in college, my philosophy professor had made of me a convinced determinist, an atheist. I suppose I had been living as such for some time, but the professor had crowned my behavior with an airtight philosophical system that could explain everything through cause and effect, or so I thought.

In 1976, before leaving for France to study French, a Catholic neighbor challenged me to rely on God for my answers. I scoffed at this idea, but one night, all alone in my French dorm, I decided to ask this God who did not exist if he existed. What he revealed next astounded me. As creator of time and space, he was not bound to these two things. He could move forward and backward as he pleased and did so for me, to demonstrate his presence. There isn't the place here to explain how he did this, but do it, he did.

I then found a choice before me. I could either reject his revelation and draw back into my fractured shell of determinism and patch it up or embrace him. I did the latter, and there never has been since that day a shadow of a doubt concerning his existence.

The following year, as a student of the University of California, Santa Barbara, I again traveled to France to spend one year studying history at the University of Bordeaux. That year transformed my life even further. In a medieval history seminar, I met Sylvie Roche, and she and I hit it off immediately, spending many hours talking family, culture, politics, and religion, and both somewhat moved by our mutual understanding of these things.

After I left Bordeaux in June of 1978, we remained friends by correspondence. In the fall of 1979, I returned to France and asked Sylvie to marry me.

If it hadn't been for Sylvie, I would not have pursued graduate studies, would not have become a professor, and would not have become an author. When we first met, I thought a scholar was someone who knew about books, she taught me to read them and to engage them in writing. She and I would go on to translate together Andre Maurois's historical fiction entitled *Neither Angel, Nor Beast*, a book with a wonderful message about the limits of social revolution that, I believe, many should consider in our tumultuous times.

Also, I think it goes without saying that had we not married, I would not have four wonderful, intelligent, and ever-entertaining children, followed by a slew of equally rewarding grandchildren.

Of course, I don't want to overstate my wife's influence. If it hadn't been for my mother, Sylvie and I would not have ended up in Nebraska, home of the Good Life: For it was my mother, who passed on to us the farm that my great-grandfather had established here in the early 1870s.

This inheritance, however, means that in addition to teaching history at a local community college, I also farm, growing corn and soybeans and raising miniature Australian shepherds. Our dogs are kind enough to share the house with us, but as often as possible, we like to give them a break by traveling abroad, especially to the British Isles, where we always go to a play or two in London and attend a church service at All Souls.

We do, from time to time, slip over into France, but mainly to visit our second son and his wife, who are in the business of making Christian films. An added bonus is that they have eight of our grandchildren and an Australian shepherd.

We would visit our first son at work, but that's often in Africa, and my Swahili is limited. It is to our advantage, then, that his home base, where he and his wife entertain various animals (horses, cats, a pig, and, of course, an Australian shepherd) is but five miles from our farm.

Fortunately, our third son only travels abroad rarely, perhaps because his Australian shepherd is very much attached to him, but when he does, we tend to be with him. Last time he took us to Dublin. Otherwise his home is located only ten miles from us, which is convenient, because it's right next door to a house inhabited by our daughter, her husband, our toddling grandson, and, of course, an Aussie.

As you can see, our children are an important part of our life, and so naturally they were the inspiration for my first novel, *The Crystal Keep*, written in the spirit of the Princess Bride, even though I had not heard of that book when I wrote mine.

My two books in historical fiction, *Life in a Casket* and *Saved by the Bullet*, were partly inspired by my granddaughter, as she, with her red hair, served as a model for my heroine. This granddaughter, I should add, being advanced in years at age 13, was also one of my editors and has edited the present work as well.

I do, of course, have another important editor and fellow writer to recognize, and that is Sylvie. So, I think it important to state that Sylvie's favorite novel of those I've written is *Knight Time for Paris*. I'm partial to it as well, because it takes me back to France and to the Middle Ages, where Sylvie and I first met.

Made in the USA
Monee, IL
03 September 2024

64415435R00204